Vasha

A Companion Novel to the EARTH'S MAGICK series

Mel Massey

Publisher's Note:

This is a work of fiction. All names, characters, places, and events are the work of the author's imagination.

Any resemblance to real persons, places, or events is coincidental.

Solstice Publishing -
www.solsticepublishing.com

VASHA

The second companion novel
To the Earth's Magick series

Mel Massey

This is dedicated to the seductive, blue devil
himself – Vasha.

EARTH'S MAGICK Series List in order:

EARTH'S MAGICK book One ~Earth~

Decker – The first companion novel

EARTH'S MAGICK book two ~Water~

Vasha – The second companion novel

EARTH'S MAGICK book three ~Fire~
(Coming soon)

Chapter One

The last of the bodies from the battle burned in a pile far from view of Mela's house. Vasha stood silent and watched the flames consume the gray flesh. It shriveled and turned black as the flames sent the creatures back to their creator. It was to *Agni* that bodies were burnt in a time long ago, in a place far from the secluded patch of woods he now found himself in. *Agni* is the messenger of the Gods and all offerings, both material and flesh, were made to him. Vasha could only hope this was the only funeral pyre he was to stand beside before this was all over.

He sighed longingly and tilted his head back to search the stars, wondering which of the ancient Gods were listening to his considerations. He knew better than to think that all of the motley crew would survive the coming war. He had witnessed too many wars. Too many deaths. For all but a select few, death was inevitable. Of that, he was certain.

***

For the next few weeks, everyone settled into a new normal. No longer would any of the inhabitants of the house go anywhere alone. No one slept unless a sentinel was arranged for the night. Vigilance, above all things, would save their lives. Or, Vasha mused, prolong them.

He arranged himself comfortably on his pile of pillows and flicked his tail. This was a small, cramped place, to be sure. However, it was the first time he had a place to call home in many, many years.

At times, the darkness of his home, dimly lit by small candles, reminded him of other places he once lived. He spent much of his life in dark seclusion so that now, when he had his freedom and ability to do as he pleased, he sought a small darkened room for comfort once more. There were times while he slept, he could recall everything about certain places he once called home. Only a few he remembered with fondness.

A knock at the door roused him from his memories. It was late afternoon. He knew Mela had not returned from work with the delectable Layla. His curiosity was piqued.

"You may enter," he spoke to the door, wondering who was on the other side.

Wyatt stuck his head inside and smiled. "Come," he waved two of his hands in the air beckoning his friend inside.

"Vasha," Wyatt closed the door behind him. Vasha watched, curious, as Wyatt came to sit on a round, yellow pillow on the floor. He carried a stack of papers, bound with metal, and a pack of pencils. "I thought you and I could have a chat."

"Oh?" Vasha's curiosity was aroused as well as his body. He enjoyed looking at the masculine figure of the man sitting before him. His hair was brown with just enough wave to make it interesting. His eyes, those beautiful hazel eyes, danced with an intoxicating mixture of knowledge and mischief. "What would you like to chat about, my treasured friend?"

"Your favorite subject. You." Wyatt said with a knowing smile and a wink. Vasha chuckled as two of his bejeweled blue arms swept hair from his face and flattened it down. His other two hands reached for the pipe and brought it to his lips.

"It is true...I am my favorite topic." Vasha said before inhaling the smoke. Wyatt smiled.

"I know. I was hoping we could do what Decker and I did, you know, talk about your history and I could write it down," he reached for one of the notebooks and opened the first page. "I've got a whole notebook just for you and your stories. If you want to tell them, that is." He said with a bit of hesitation.

Vasha exhaled the smoke in a delicate line towards the ceiling watching Wyatt as he did. "And what do I get for telling you all of my deepest secrets?"

Wyatt laughed and looked down at the paper, then back up. "Immortality." He said.

"Oh…well, I seem to already possess that. Do you care to raise the wager a little?"

"My undying gratitude and the knowledge that your story will be written down and, no matter what happens, the world will always have record of you." Wyatt said.

Vasha considered Wyatt's words and watched the man. He was so lovely. He would take great pleasure in him if given the chance.

"Of course, I would love to impart my history to you. I have offered it in the past, if you remember. However, you were busy with my brother at the time."

"Yeah, I thought it was best to go to him first." Wyatt said with a knowing look.

Vasha smiled slowly then nodded. "A shrewd decision. My brother, for as much as I love him, has a fragile sense of self. You were wise to go to him first. It made him happy, and," he inhaled more smoke. "Gave Theo and myself the opportunity to know him better." He blew the smoke out. "For that, I thank you."

"Great. If you've got time now, I'm free. Annabelle is playing with Theo for a bit. They really get along well."

"Yes, my brother has always had a soft spot for the young and forgotten. She is in good hands."

"I agree. Now," he began writing on the paper and looked up at Vasha expectantly. "I know about what year you were born. From my notes after talking to Decker," he checked the penciled dates and read it aloud. "Close to three hundred years before the common era. That sound about right to you?"

Vasha shrugged. "If you say so. My tale begins the same as my brothers'; however, once I left our little cave by the valley my life took a very different turn."

"Okay. But something confuses me…"

"Already? Oh dear." Vasha said with a smile while Wyatt laughed.

"Decker said that, after Azul took off, you were the next to go and that you," he checked his paper again to ensure he was correct. "Took off in the middle of the night along with almost everything in the home. That right?"

"It is." He answered with a nod.

"Why?"

"Why did I leave? Or why did I take all of our things?"

"Both."

"I left because my sisters were gone. I missed them so. I was young. Far younger in both years and maturity than my brethren. I needed my sisters, you see. I have always needed someone to care for me. It is my flaw." He said holding out his arms.

"You don't have any flaws, Vasha." Wyatt teased.

"You flatter me. Nevertheless, I was simply sad. That was a confusing time for me, you understand. The Darkness had bewitched us so thoroughly that I no longer trusted my sisters or my brothers. I felt truly alone. When I left, I was angry. I was the only one who cared about the lovely rugs they made for us. Or the pretty baskets they spent all day weaving. It was a petty thing, I grant you, but there it is." He leaned to the side and tucked another pillow beneath him.

"I see. So, you left one night while they slept, from what Decker said. Where did you go first?" Wyatt asked with his pencil poised over the paper prepared to write.

Vasha sat back, his eyes narrowing in thought. "Decker's history is filled with adventure and war, is it not? Mine, mine is filled with a whole other type of thing. Are you certain you wish to hear what I have to tell you?"

"Yes."

"Very well, I shall hold nothing back from you. I am not ashamed of my past nor do I wish for any of it to have turned out any different. I am thankful, you see, for the life I have lived. It has made me into the beast I am today."

"Why do you call yourself a beast?"

He smiled. "Why not? I am, my darling, a beast of the worst sort. You will see why I say this, if my physique does not already prove it to you."

"I'm ready when you are. I'm not scared, you blue devil." He said with a wink.

"Very well, but you must promise me one thing," Wyatt nodded. "You will not judge me on what I tell you of my past. I, like all others walking this earth, have made grave mistakes. I request that you do not hold this against me."

"Scout's honor." Wyatt said and crossed his heart with his finger.

"What a peculiar pledge. You asked of the night I left, yes?" Wyatt nodded and began to write. Vasha took a hefty puff from his long pipe and blew the smoke into delicate rings. "I traveled from my first home with a sense of excitement and wonder. For I had never been beyond the valley that lay at the foot of our cave home. Unlike Decker, I cannot pass as human, even for an instant. I cannot fly as Azul and Theo can. I was, shall we say, pampered and sheltered. My sisters catered to my every need all my short life, and I thought it was time I cared for myself. How very wrong I was."

Vasha adjusted his pose on the pillows. Now that he was finally telling this story, a feeling of nervousness settled in. It was a foreign feeling and he allowed it to wash over him.

"I remember, I traveled only by night. I had a vague curiosity to see the sea that lay to our northeast. I could smell the air the closer I travelled to the water, fish and salt are heavy fragrances. I care not for them."

"I like the smell of the ocean." Wyatt said as he wrote in his notebook.

"To each his own, I suppose. However, it was a fascinating time for me. The world was brand new and I, I was a creature unknown even to myself. I slept in caves along the seaside, enjoyed the sound of the sea and delighted in the seagulls that flew in the early morning light. My very first encounter with humans, other than my sisters, were a band of merchants I believe. They camped on the beach one night and I remember watching them for a long time. They looked so different from myself. I stayed in my cave and listened to them speak. I admired the robes of different colors they wore. One even had a gold necklace that I craved desperately. It was then that I got the wild idea that I wished to find others like myself."

"Did you know if there were others like you? Or were you just hoping?" Wyatt asked.

"Both. I hoped and I felt as though there must be. Do you understand this? Perhaps, I wanted it to be so badly, that I convinced myself it was true. Whatever the reason, as I watched the men leave the following morning, I resolved to not be alone any longer. I would find others like myself. I wanted to see more of the beautifully colored robes and gold. Oh…how I love gold." He lovingly caressed the delicate bracelets that ran up and down his arms.

"I can tell."

"You do not know the half of it. It was my love for gold that brought me to my very first, shall we say, adventure." He took a long puff of smoke and closed his eyes, remembering the faces of those long dead. "I journeyed for many moon turns. You understand this, yes?" Wyatt shook his head no. "We did not have scheduled days, as you have them now. Your life is very programmed. It confuses me," he waved his hands in the air to chase away his confusion. "We simply counted the passing of time by the moon's phases. A New Moon was a black night then it would grow in the sky to a full moon. Then it would again fade. This would signal a monthly cycle, as you know it now."

"Ah, I see." Wyatt scribbled in his notebook as Vasha looked on with a smile.

"One night, after having traveled for many turns of the moon," he inclined his head to Wyatt who nodded his understanding. "I saw a wondrous thing. After seeing nothing but the sea, sand, and seagulls, I finally saw my very first wonder. Silk tents sat like small castles in the sand by the shore. Of course, they were not truly castles but to my inexperienced eyes, they were a wonder. There were several tents, made of colored silk, surrounded by torches that danced in the sea air. Oh, it was beautiful, Wyatt. From somewhere inside there were drums playing and I longed to get closer. I could smell fragrances I never before smelled. Perfumes and food mingled together. It was intoxicating."

"I can't imagine such a thing after living in a cave your entire life. It's like the Mother Ship was calling you home." Wyatt joked.

"A mother ship? No. It was not a ship but tents."

"I know that... I... never mind. Keep going." Wyatt laughed and wrote more in his notebook.

"I lingered long listening to the tantalizing rhythms of the drums. My mouth watered at the delectable smells coming from within. People were walking this way and that, but no one saw me as I hid behind rocks. It was night and the moon was not full, so there was little chance of being discovered. Or so I thought."

"Someone saw you?" Wyatt looked up from his writing.

"Patience. I will get to it, my eager boy. Where was I? Oh yes, I was hiding. It was then I realized that the people I had seen thus far were merely servants. They wore beautiful, white robes and were very clean, you see. However, when they opened the silken drapes and more people came from within, I was captivated. The men wore mantles of the most beautiful cloth could even imagine. Blues and yellows...

deep red and gold. So much gold they wore. Even on their toes there were tiny jewels set in gold. I wanted these people in what way I could not begin to tell you. I was as a moth to the flame. I could not help myself as I crept from behind my hiding place to get closer to the lovely humans. That was when I saw the women. They followed behind the men, speaking to one another in hushed tones. Their dark brown skin peeked out from beneath colorful, silken robes. They too were covered head to toe in gold trinkets. Their hair, it was their hair that caused my pulse to quicken and to feel joy in my heart."

"Why their hair? What was so special about it?"

"It was like mine, you see. Long, black, and shimmering. My hair is beautiful, is it not?" Vasha asked, shaking head to make his raven locks ripple over his shoulders. Wyatt smiled and nodded his head. "Only one of my sisters had black hair, but it was not the same. I was, and continue to be, an oddity among my family."

"I think you're all odd actually." Wyatt said.

"So it would seem," Vasha said. "I crept closer until I was barely in the shadows. I was dangerously close to the women as they gathered around a torch held by a servant. Their voices were unlike anything I had ever heard before. They were refined, you see. These women in their flowing robes, scarves of different colors, and sparkling gold jewelry were the most exotic sight I had ever seen."

"Sounds like quite the beach party."

"It was. However, in my inexperience at life, the guards saw me. Before I knew it, men with swords drawn surrounded me and they were yelling. '*What is it?*' loudly. The women screamed at the monster that was lurking so close to them. Everywhere, there were men with swords and lances, ready to put an end to me."

"Were you scared?"

"A little, I admit it. I spent my life hiding and was never seen by another living soul. I knew I was different. However, it was not until that night that I saw what my sisters hid from me. They sheltered me from the fear and natural hatred that comes along with such a fear. I saw myself, for the first time, through their eyes. I was a monster in the dark to them. I was a thing to be feared."

"What happened?"

"Before I could do anything, they had me tied in ropes and dragged like an animal to the feet of the one in charge. The women cowered behind the men as I lay panting from fear and pain from the ropes. I remember seeing a man's feet in the sand. He wore jeweled sandals and his robes were colorful. He stood over me and spoke to his guards to sit me up. They did as was bid. Then the man came close and bent low to see me up close. Oh, he was a fine man. Saracan was his name. He quietly looked me over from head to tail, studying me with his dark eyes. He had lovely eyes, my sweet Saracan.

"I spent the night tied like an animal, surrounded by men. However, Saracan would step out of his tent and regard me with his lovely eyes, then return to the colorful palace of silk. Many times he did this. Can you guess why?"

"He was curious?"

"Oh, he was indeed. I am a curiosity, am I not? Saracan was afraid. This was a man with a deep sense of honor. He was a believer in the old Gods and did not wish to anger them. What he must have thought, sweet Saracan…"

"The way you say his name, you and he were friends?"

"Of a sort," Vasha reached behind him and rummaged through a large chest, only to pull out a smaller box. He spoke as he rummaged around inside. "Saracan came out of his tent one last time. He carried a torch and sat a few feet from me, much as you are. He crossed his legs in the sand and studied me. I made no moves that would scare him. I desperately wanted the beautiful man to love me. Before long, he inched his way closer until he was close enough to touch. Of course, I could have ripped the ropes from my hands had I known my own strength then. But I did not, you see. I was frightened and desperate."

"Kind of makes me sad for you…" Wyatt said as he scribbled away in his notebook.

"I am sad for the young me as well. So much of the world and human nature had been hidden from me. Before long, Saracan reached out to touch me and I held as still as a statue. I wanted him to know he had no reason to fear me. Then, he spoke. I remember the way his voice sounds as though it were yesterday. His was a proper man's voice. It was deep and gentle."

"What did he say?"

"He asked me, '*Did the Gods send you to me?*' Naturally, I said yes."

"You said yes?"

"I would have admitted to anything at that moment. When I answered him, he nodded his head as though he suspected it all along. He said I was the answer to the problem and called for his guards."

"What problem?"

"I did not know, nor did I care. All I cared about was that the ropes were no longer tying my hands together. They left one long rope around my neck and showed me to the largest tent in the caravan. It was a deep blue with fine linen hanging from the parapets. I had never seen such beauty. I followed like a good pet because I did not want them to turn me away. Saracan took my rope and instructed the guards to leave us alone. There, he offered me food and drink. I did my best to eat with the proper manners my sisters taught me. I thanked him for his hospitality and he was pleased. Such delicacies he offered me…olives, mushrooms with peppers, chickpeas swimming in oil and garlic. It was a wondrous night for me."

"I'm sure it was for him too." Wyatt said with a chuckle.

"It was. For Saracan, he dined with a messenger of the Gods. I presented myself in such a way that allowed him to believe I was at his mercy. For that, he gave me food and a safe place to sleep. I spent the night in his tent and watched as Saracan fell asleep watching me with his lovely dark eyes."

"Did you leave? While they were all asleep?"

"No, dear boy. Why in the world would I do such a thing? No, I was a proper beast and stayed where my master left me. I slept little that night as I was most excited. I passed the time wondering what sort of life I would have there, living by the sea in our silken tents. However, when the morning came, so did my education."

"Uh oh."

"In the morning, I ate once again with Saracan. We dined on dates with honey, fresh loaves of bread, baked fish from the sea, and peppered nuts. It was delightful."

"But what was he going to do with you? Weren't you worried at all? I mean, these were strangers and they could have hurt you." Wyatt frowned as he spoke.

"Your concern for me is touching, Wyatt. Rest assured, I always ensure that, regardless of what the Fates have in store for me, I come out triumphant."

"Sorry. It just seems scary."

"Certainly. I understand. Now, after we ate, Saracan brought the other men into the tent and explained to them that I was an omen from the Gods. He instructed them to prepare a palanquin for me and that I was returning with them. This was a surprise to me, you see, as I naively thought we were to live in the tents by the sea."

"Where were they going to take you? Did they say?"

"No. They did not say just then and I could not ask. You see, if I was to play out the ruse of being a messenger of the Gods, I had to pretend I was already aware of their intentions. So, I sat as demurely as possible, nodding and smiling at all the right times. Before long, the servants were rushing back and forth packing Saracan's belongings. Saracan himself groomed me for the trip. He washed my feet in a bowl of water. He brushed my hair and dabbed scented oils all over me until I smelled as fine as he. Then," Vasha held something out to show Wyatt. "He handed me this. It was once wrapped in a golden scarf, but that has since fallen to pieces." Vasha held up a long chain necklace made of solid gold. The pendant that hung was the size of an egg. It was an uneven flattened piece of gold with flecks of rubies around the edge. In the middle were etchings that Wyatt could not understand.

"What does it say?" he asked in awe.

"The spirit of the tiger. Some talisman Saracan carried that he thought was of some significance. I did not care what it said at the time. I fell in love with the feel and weight of the gold around my neck. However, to my Saracan, I was the embodiment of the tiger and an answer to his prayer. He had left the palace, searching for some grand sign from the Gods to bring back to the Emperor. What he found was me."

"The Emperor?"

"Oh yes. That is where they were taking me. I overheard the servants talking. I learned to listen and I learned then that the servants were the very best source of information. That little lesson served me very well down the road. But I get ahead of myself..." Vasha placed the gold necklace around his neck and stared at the engraved piece in his hands. "I remember Saracan saying to me as he led me to my palanquin, *'Perhaps you will help bring things to right. Perhaps at the sight of you, the Gods will return to us'.*"

"What did he mean by that?"

"I did not know at the time. I did not care. I smiled my foolish smile and followed along as the servants lowered the palanquin and bowed as I climbed inside. I liked that. Inside were soft pillows, much like you see in here," he caressed one of the pillows on the floor. "I was finally on my own and had found someone with kind eyes to take care of me. The servants cared for all of my belongings. A young boy whose name I cannot remember now catered to all of my needs. I only remember he was small and had a tight gold chain around his neck. I envied his golden chain then. It was only when it was too late did I realize I too would have my own chains once I met the Emperor."

"Golden chains?"

"No," Vasha settled back, his expression became unusually somber. "Beasts were not given golden chains."

"How long was the trip in the palanquin?"

"Oh, perhaps a fortnight. Maybe more. I cannot recall the details of that sort of thing. I ate well. I was blissfully unaware of my fate even as we approached the gates to the city. Saracan came to whisper through the gauze that covered my palanquin, '*Do not open the drapes, blessed one. We must keep you a secret'*."

Wyatt frowned, "Sounds fishy."

"Perhaps if I were as shrewd as yourself, I would have felt a desire to run then. As I should have. I could see some of the city as we passed through it. People were everywhere talking, laughing, singing… it was the most beautiful thing I had ever seen. Nothing, short of a cave full of gold could have torn me away from Saracan then. I saw real children playing games together. I saw women fetching water from the wells. I wanted them all. I remember as the servants carried the palanquins up many stone stairs, that I could see that more of the city lay beneath me. I admit, I did peek through the gauze a few times." Vasha laughed.

"Can't say that I blame you. So, Saracan was taking you to the Emperor. Do you remember his name at all?"

Vasha's face once again took on a dark look. "Yes. I remember his name all too well. But allow me to tell you of the beauty that I experienced before I tell you of my pain. You see, it is important to remember both. Beauty and pain often times go together. One cannot eclipse the other."

"Sure, sorry. Go on."

Vasha closed his eyes as he spoke. "I remember the smells of the palace. Lingering aromas of food mixed with the heady scent of Myrrh and Lavender. All around my palanquin, servants stood blocking any possible view of me inside. I heard many people walking about and speaking in hushed tones. Then, I was carried further into the palace. Down long hallways we went… I seem to remember there were many lit torches that we passed. It must have been heavy to carry me for such a long way. Funny, I'd never considered that before." Vasha chuckled as he brought the pipe to his lips.

"Where did they take you?"

"To a large room. It was by far my favorite room of what I saw of the palace.

The walls were covered in gold. Images of winged creatures, much like my brothers, and myself stood in relief on the stone. Once they permitted me to step from the palanquin, I was drunk on the beauty of the place. Jewels decorated the images on the walls. As the servants passed them carrying torches, the very walls glittered and seemed to move in the shadows." Wyatt waited silently with his pencil poised over the paper for Vasha to continue. "He came from one of the antechamber doors. His servants surrounded him and Saracan walked slightly to the side. I stood tall and proud as my eyes fell upon the Emperor. He was of average height with black hair and a sharp angle to his nose that most men in that part of the world possess. His garments were fine, so very fine. And of course, gold hung from around his neck and adorned every part of him that I could see. His guards wore yellow... I remember that now. Their uniforms were the color of gold."

"What happened next?" Wyatt asked breathlessly.

"My Saracan stepped between us and grandly gestured towards me while he faced the Emperor. '*A gift for you, your Highness. A sign from the Gods has come to bless you.*' He was so proud, my beloved Saracan. The Emperor, with his hands clasped behind his back, stepped closer to me and took in every detail. I remember hoping he thought me lovely. I wished for him to embrace me. I needed this man, this Emperor, to love me."

"Did he?"

"In his way…" he cleared his throat before he continued. "Darrius was his name. He looked me over in silence then stood and stared into my eyes. I wondered at him then. I thought he was a terribly brave man to stand before me so fearless. I thought he must be a great ruler to be so brave. But alas… he was not a great man. He was a great tyrant, as I soon learned." Vasha leaned forward and reached out toward Wyatt with all four of his arms extended. "Do you see? Look here, my lovely one," One delicate blue finger pointed to his wrists, his voice urgent. "Do you see them now?"

"Scars?" Wyatt whispered, too afraid of the alarming ferocity in Vasha's voice.

"Yes. Scars. Scars I earned over many, many years in the service of Darrius, King of the Achaemid Empire."

"I don't understand-"

"Do you not? I thought I would be a loved member of the royal family… how foolish I was then. After Darrius finished looking me over, he whispered to his guards something that I could not hear. Of course, I was so foolish, I did not even pay attention. I watched as Saracan's face fell and wondered what made him so sad all of a sudden. I was a stupid thing."

"What did Darrius whisper to his guards, Vasha?" Wyatt asked in a soft voice.

Vasha sat back and lit the pipe that had long since gone out and puffed two then three times before he was satisfied with the cloud of smoke around him. "Before I knew what was happening, the guards in yellow surrounded me and pointed their spears at my throat. I was most terrified. I looked in vain for my Saracan but he could not intervene. The Emperor barked orders and they poked me in the back until I stepped forward. From another room an old man came. When he saw me, his terror was plain. He nearly dropped the jar in his hands. With my Saracan begging the Emperor for mercy and the guards poking me with their spears, I felt the very first wave of desperation come over me. I felt the animal within. For a moment, I could have torn them all apart. I should have… it would have saved much pain had I simply dispatched them all that day."

"What stopped you?"

Vasha let out an empty laugh. "I still thought it something I could remedy with good behavior and a smile. I thought, perhaps if I show them I am docile and will do as I am told, they will let me live. As I said, I was a foolish thing."

"Not foolish, you were hopeful. Innocent."

"Innocent. Yes. That I was. But soon, they were forcing a foul-smelling drink down my throat and the room began to spin. I fell forward and my head hit the floor. It was a beautiful floor but it had no warmth. It was as cold as a snake's skin. For that was where I found myself, in a snake pit. When I awoke," he puffed on his pipe again and extended his arms once more. "I was chained in a dark room. It was cold and wet. I could smell many foul things all around me as I came to."

"Why? Why did he do it?"

"He was a mad man. You should read your history books, young Wyatt. He is in them and his legacy is not near as torrid as the actual man. The real Darrius is far worse than the one you will read about. Here, I will tell you all now. For I am in a foul mood as I think of him. It is best we get past this and to more pleasant things." Vasha settled down into his pillows. The memories played in his mind and a glimmer of the beast shone through for a moment shattering the usual calm and tenacious exterior. His lips curled up showing the sharp canines he would normally hide behind a smirk.

"He hurt you then? This Darrius the King?"

"Oh… we were to call him Emperor. In truth, he was simply a King. But when Darrius wanted a thing… he would have it. He believed I was a messenger from the Gods, that much Saracan got right. What he had not accounted for was Darrius's hatred for them. I believe he was angry he himself was not a God. He thought, what better way to hurt them than to humiliate and torment their beloved messenger? I could not tell them then that I was not, you see. No one would believe me. I endured… much pain. He would wake in the morning and, after his meal, he would come to the dark room where he kept me. The young boy that was his torchbearer would stand silently as Darius would whip me. He had many tools of choice, but he preferred a simple long string of leather with golden hooks at the end. It tore the flesh better that way."

"My God…"

"I did not have a God then. No one came to rescue me. Every evening, the old man would come and force the foul drink down my throat. I spent hours drugged. Then beaten. Then drugged. Then beaten again. I lost track of the days. Saracan came to see me after some time. He brought his son… I do not remember his name. He was barely a man and I was barely alive. Saracan cried and begged my forgiveness. He tore his shirt and cried to the Gods for help. He swore he would see me free. It was he who sent to me my one and only friend in the palace. Her name was Stateira. She was a lovely, doe-eyed thing. She was one of Darrius's daughters. He had no interest in women, other than to create an heir. I am not certain when Stateira began to come. I only remember that she was there in the beginning. She would feed me from her own fingers. Once she knew I would not harm her, she began to treat my wounds and whisper softly to me songs that I cannot remember now. I only remember her sweet voice and the soft touch of her hands as she dabbed herbs into my wounds."

"How long did this go on?"

"I am not certain of many things about that time. It was all… foggy. Do you understand this? I was fed opiates every evening. Whipped every morning. Between the pain and the drugs, I did not know myself anymore. Only Stateira came to comfort me. I remember… her pretty face," One blue hand ran down his face, the golden bracelets on his arms were the only sound in the shed. "I remember better when the fighting started. For the Emperor was called away to lead his armies."

"Fighting? Who was fighting who?"

"Alexander had arrived. Do you read the history books, my beloved?" Wyatt nodded. "Then you know anyone who stood before Alexander eventually fell. So, it was with Darrius. My first captor." Vasha sighed and readjusted himself on the pillows. "I was in a terrible state when Darrius finally met his well-earned end. I was still in my dark room when Saracan came in, Stateira on his heels. She comforted me, tears on her cheeks, as she softly kissed my cheeks. *'It is over, blessed one. We shall see you freed soon.'* But, the Fates had other plans for me. I was in no fit state to go anywhere. I was addicted to the foul drink and had been chained too long. I no longer had a will to live. I wanted death. As you and I both know, death does not find my kind easily."

"What happened then? If Darrius was dead, couldn't Saracan or Stateira help you? Did they at least unchain you?"

Vasha shook his head. "No. I was unfit to be let lose. I do believe, in my weakened and drugged state, I would have done much damage. I knew they discussed with the old man limiting the amount of the Opiates in my drink until it was all but gone from my system. They had a plan, you see.

To tame me once more. I was no longer having my flesh torn from my body every morning. That made me quite docile as you can imagine. However, it was the desire for the drug that caused the most pain. For weeks, I lay chained to the wet floor, sweating, and crying out for more. But Stateira would bring a cold cloth and wipe the sweat from my face. My wounds were almost healed by the time I felt more myself. It must have taken weeks and weeks to see me through that darkness."

"At least."

"Saracan came one night to bring me my dinner. He had unchained one hand so that I could now feed myself. It took me many attempts. I had not had the full use of my arms in so long, I thought them all but limp weights forever. But… I recovered."

"At least you had a friend. I don't know how you managed to survive and come out… well… normal."

Vasha's face relaxed into laughter. "It took many, many years for me to regain myself but we are not there yet. We must still travel through the darkness a while more. You see, my troubles, I thought, were over with the death of Darrius. However, word soon came to Saracan to prepare my beloved Stateira for marriage to the man that killed her father."

"No."

"Indeed. Those were the times in which we lived. When beasts pretended to be men and men pretended not to be beasts."

"You're such a poet." Wyatt said with a soft smile.

"I once dabbled in poetry. However, I lost interest after a time as I am want to do." Vasha placed the long pipe to the side and stared hard at the gold necklace from so long ago. "I cannot remember the last time I wore this piece. The memories it brings…. I remember the smell of the dark room they kept me in. I remember the pain I felt. I remember so much when I see this…"

"If this is too painful, we can take a break if you want."

Vasha smiled a sad smile. "No, my dear one. Those who caused me pain are long dead. Their bones now dust. Where were we?"

"They were marrying Stateira to Alexander. That really happened?"

"Oh yes," Vasha tore his gaze from the necklace and settled back against his pile of pillows. "It did indeed happen. She was so nervous, the pretty thing. She would visit me after her morning meal and comb my hair for me. She told me how afraid she was of being a wife. Now remember," he leaned in toward his friend, "These were different times. Stateira was to be his second wife. Although beautiful, and well-bred, hers was a marriage of alliance. A necessary evil as Saracan pointed out time and time again."

"I understand."

"Good," he nodded his elegant head. "I was quite a bit better by the time Stateira was forced to wed Alexander. I did not go to the wedding nor did I ever lay eyes on the man. I wish I had. I missed many interesting things locked away as I was. After the wedding, Stateira came to see me even more often. I would ask her as she bathed me and braided my hair, why she was not with her new husband? *'He has gone off again to fight in another war.'* The young thing was very sad. Even more now that her father was dead and she had married a wealthy warrior. I thought, being second wife cannot be all that bad, can it? I was unaware of the torment she herself endured even as she cared for me in my darkest time."

"Alexander was mean to her?"

"No, not Alexander. But his first wife. Roxana. It took many weeks for Stateira to finally divulge her own pain to me. She sat by my side, weeping like a child and told me of how Roxana beat her with a stick. How she yelled horrible things to her constantly. You see, she was a docile thing after surviving her father after all. She had perfected the art of invisibility to many but to the jealous eyes of Roxana, who saw her youth and beauty, she became a target. What was more, any children Stateira and Alexander had together could threaten the claim of Roxana's children after Alexander's death."

"Oh, I see. The poor thing."

"Yes. The poor thing," Vasha's face changed while. His eyes moved back and forth as he recalled the details. "Because Alexander was constantly at war, Stateira had all the more reason to disappear from her tormentor and sit with me in my dark room. She brought oil lamps and blankets for me. I loved the colorful linens so she brought me spools full. My Stateira was a skilled seamstress. She made me clothes in the fashion of her people. Of course, it is next to impossible for me to wear clothes but I liked the tunics just fine. It was her company that soothed me the most. Her mild manner and sweet voice reminded me… she reminded me of my sisters. Even in looks she resembled them.

"She aided me in my recovery and in months I was walking about. She could not remove the chains from my neck but I did not complain. I had faith my Saracan would find a place for me soon. I dreamt of a time when I could live in the castle as a free creature. I wished for servants and a room with golden walls. How very foolish I was then."

"What happened, Vasha? What happened to Stateira?"

"How very perceptive of you, Wyatt. When word came to the Palace that Alexander had been killed in battle, many did not believe it was true. How could they? He had gone undefeated for so long. The son of Zeus himself, as some liked to say. Stateira was concerned with good reason. Roxana was in a rage and had her own worries. If Alexander was indeed dead, she was an outsider and at extreme risk in this foreign place.

"I remember the night before… Stateira was with me, reading something aloud. I do not remember what. It was boring but I enjoyed her voice so I did not voice my displeasure. Saracan came as well. He smiled and showed me what he held in his hand. It was the key to my chains. The chain around my neck was no longer holding me against the wall. I was as free as I had been in a long time. Stateira and I were happy that night. We fanaticized about sharing rooms in the Palace once Roxana was gone. We laughed and I even sang a song with her."

Vasha's eyes filled with tears and he looked down once again to the gold necklace that sealed his fate so long ago. One of his hands moved to wipe the tears away. "During the night," His voice cracked and Wyatt had never heard it so deep. "During the night I heard screams. I knew it was Stateira because she called for me. I heard her calling for me from somewhere overhead. It did not take me long to rip the door from its frame. I ran swiftly up dark stairs. I believe I fell once or twice. I was not accustomed to running in quite some time. I was slow and clumsy.

"I saw lights finally and followed those. I could no longer hear Stateira. The lights hurt my eyes but I kept moving. Like a wraith, I moved through the torch lit halls until I could smell her scent. I remembered myself then. Nose down low, I followed the smell and it took me up higher and higher into the castle. I am unsure even to this day if anyone saw me moving about. If they did, I must have been quite frightful to see."

"I've seen you do your thing. You're pretty scary to us regular people."

"Indeed. Regular people."

"I didn't mean anything by that-"

Vasha held up his hand. "I know what you meant. I was agreeing with you. Fear not," he smiled. "Back to this dark tale... I ran until I reached large double doors. On the other side was Stateira. I hesitated because I did not want her to be angry with me for leaving the dark room but she had called for me, hadn't she?

"I listened with my face close to the door but I heard nothing except a woman crying. Finally, it was the scent of blood that filled my nose that caused me to crash through the wooden doors. The woman, Roxana, was seated on a cushion crying into her hands. She screamed when I came in. I was not concerned with her, however. It was the sight of my beloved Stateira lying in a pool of blood that caused me to cry out. It was a horrible cry. The beast within me mourned so much... I could not hold it in. I picked her up and held her against me. Her body was already cold. I asked Roxana, *'Who did this thing to her?'* The foul woman stood up and threw her pillow at me. *'Be gone, creature! She is of no use to anyone now! I killed the wretched girl. I will rule in my husband's place.'*

"I carefully placed my one and only friend back on the floor and stood to my full height as I faced Roxana. She cowered from me but I am faster than regular people," he gave Wyatt a sad smile. "I wrapped two hands around her neck and the other two held her arms by her side. I screamed at her.

I remember that. I shook her and called her horrible things. With Stateira's blood still on my hands, I slammed Roxana's head against the wall. Over and over again until I heard her skull crack and her body went limp."

"Jesus…"

"She deserved that death. I do not apologize for it. I carried my darling friend from that woman's room and placed her in her own bed. Roxana had stabbed her in the throat and her passing was horrific. Her delicate face was serene in death."

"Is that when you left? You left the Palace, didn't you?"

"No. I did not. I stayed by Stateira's side and wept like a child. It was Saracan who found me before the guards could. They would have killed me or made an attempt at any rate. I cried so as Saracan swept me from the room, urging me along with his soft words. I would have followed him anywhere. His was the only kind voice left in the world to me. He took me back to my dark room. There, he cleaned the blood from my hands in silence. I knew Stateira's death caused him pain. Nevertheless, he tended to me despite the tears in his eyes. When he was finished, he placed a chaste kiss on my cheek, '*It is time you left us, Vashanu. I have made plans with another, more worthy kingdom to care for you. Rest now and all will be well.'*

"I know my beloved Saracan meant well for me. I am certain of it. However, where I went after I left the Palace of Darrius was a whole other nightmare. Perhaps," he leaned forward and rested his head in his hands. "We should save this part of the tale for another night. I must confess, Wyatt, I am taxed far more than I thought I would be. These memories bring such melancholy to my heart."

"Of course. I understand. I'll just go and check on Annabelle and Theo."

"Unless," Vasha smiled slyly. "You'd like to offer some measure of comfort to me?"

"Oh, you," Wyatt swatted playfully at Vasha's hand that reached out to him. "I have big boy things to do. I can't just sit around and dilly dally with you all day. I've got responsibilities."

"I wasn't suggesting simply sitting around."

"I know what you were suggesting."

"Very well. Leave me alone in my pain," Wyatt groaned and rolled his eyes. "I will see you soon, yes? You will return for more?"

"Yes. Tomorrow?"

"Until then." Wyatt waved and closed the door softly behind him.

Vasha sat in silence for a few moments before sitting upright. As if seized with a sudden frantic desire, he opened chest after chest, digging through their contents. His breath came faster with each chest he searched. Had he thrown it away? After all this time? It had been so long since he had seen it…

Finally, in one of the smaller, much older boxes within one of the chests, he found what he was looking for. He held it deftly in his hands and sat back down on his pillows ignoring the mess he made.

He held the small bundle to his nose and inhaled deeply. Very little, if any, trace of her scent remained on it. If it did, it was most likely his imagination. He felt the once soft linen and rubbed his fingers against it. It was frail, hard, and the yellow color was all but faded. Carefully so as not to tear it, he placed it on the floor and gently unfolded the material. The yellow on the cloth was a bit brighter on the inside. His breath caught in his chest when he saw the dark rust color on the inside. This was her blood. That night when he placed her on her bed, her deathbed, he tore a strip of cloth from her clothes. Why he kept it all this time, he did not know. He sat and stared at the relic before him.

She was long dead. He had not thought of the doe-eyed girl in so long but he could not tell his story without mentioning her. She was not a great love such as his brother's wife was to him. Stateira showed him kindness when he desperately needed it. Her death was the first of many he witnessed over his long life but losing her traumatized him most deeply, worse even than being held captive. Hers was the first soul that ever looked upon him with love and affection that was not one of his brothers or sisters.

She was his first friend.

Chapter Two

Vasha slept fitfully. His dreams were full of the voices of the dead. By the time morning crept over the wall of trees that surrounded their little home, he was awake setting the chests and their contents back to right.

He spent the day walking about Mela's backyard, sullen and brooding. He avoided conversation as much as possible with the others. Inside him, old wounds were uncovered and pain from long ago filled his chest. He wallowed in it. He let it fill him and with the pain came more vivid memories. Theo hovered nearby. He could feel him waiting for an invitation to speak of the pain he was carrying.

Vasha wished to keep the pain inside, releasing it only once for Wyatt to witness and record. Later, after his time Wyatt was concluded, he would impart his tale to his brothers. Not yet though. Not yet. The delicious pain made him feel alive. Pleasure and pain were so alike. He watched as Mela and Bear walked toward the other

Witches in the field. They were doing some sort of magicks on the land surrounding the house. It was a good idea. However, he could not help them even if he wanted to. He smiled as he watched Owen watch Mela. That young man had a deep well of affection for his little Witch. He knew it the moment the three of them first met in his shed. The way the boy looked at her, eyes full of desire, ready to fall at her feet with the slightest inclination from her. Mela was ignorant to his affections. The kiss they shared had not been repeated, much to everyone's disappointment.

He turned to see the three Witches walking shoulder to shoulder into the woods followed closely by the dog Bear and the annoying bird, Teagan. Vasha turned back to his shed but stopped short. Decker was on the porch, holding a cup of some spirits, no doubt, as he too watched the Witches disappear.

Chuckling to himself, Vasha entered his shed and closed the door behind him.

***

"Yoohoo!" Wyatt called out.

"You may enter—" Vasha caught himself just in time before Annabelle entered the room. "Why hello, dear one. How are you this fine evening?"

Annabelle walked calmly toward Vasha and wrapped her arms around his neck. "I'm good, Uncle Vasha. Guess what? I'm going to go to school! A real school with other kids and everything." Wyatt entered then with a smile.

"That's right. My little Princess is off to the third grade. Got everything finalized this afternoon." Wyatt smiled like a proud father.

"Then congratulations are in order to our future scholar," Vasha said with a smile. "Perhaps a token of congratulations?" He turned and opened the chest nearest to him. "I believe I have just the thing for a proper princess…"

"What is it?" Annabelle whispered in awe.

"You don't have to, Vasha."

Vasha waved him off then turned toward Annabelle once again. "Here, little one. A gift to commemorate your first day of studies like a proper lady." One of his hands held hers open as another placed a delicate gold chain in her hands.

"Oh," Annabelle said as she stared with wide eyes at her hands.

"She's just a little girl, Vasha." Wyatt chided him.

"I will hear no more. It is special to me, just as she is." He turned back to Annabelle. "When you wear it, think of me there beside you protecting you and cheering you on, you lovely girl. Go," he kissed her forehead. "Off with you now. My brother awaits his favorite playmate." She wrapped her frail little arms around his neck once more and kissed his cheek.

"I love you, Uncle Vasha. I don't care what anyone says, I don't think you're inappropriate at all." And with that, she scampered from the room, her fist clinched tightly around the golden necklace.

Wyatt flashed his dazzling smile and took his seat across from Vasha.

"How will her transition be? Is she ready to go to school?" Vasha asked with a slight tilt of the head.

Wyatt exhaled loudly and ran his hand through his perfectly coiffed hair. "I wanted to wait but Renee, the nurse from her old hospital, said it was time. She's adjusting well and the last appointment with her doctor went well too. Everyone agrees it'll be the best thing for her. I just… I don't know."

"You are afraid for her."

"Yes," Wyatt nodded. "I'm terrified. What if it's the wrong thing to do? What if we missed something? What if she goes and freaks out when I leave her all alone?"

"My dear boy, you are experiencing what one would call parenthood."

"It's so hard, Vasha. And so wonderful all at the same time."

"Do you regret your decision? To take in this odd child as your own?"

"God no," he shook his head firmly. "I don't regret a thing. I just didn't know it would be so... I didn't know it would feel like this."

Vasha toyed with a bright green scarf and smiled, "The best things in life make you feel incredible pain. Did you know that? It is not the moments when we get everything we want that make us grow and learn, but the painful memories. Your pain and worry for the girl is normal and an important part of being a father, Wyatt. Rest easy, you are doing a fine job." He reached out to pat Wyatt's hand.

"Thank you," he pulled his notebook out and opened it to the page where he had left off the night before. His handwriting was small but very neat. On the margins of the papers were scribbled dates and notations of numbers. "Now, you left off last night when Saracan told you he had found a new place for you. Are you ready to continue telling that part? If it's too hard—"

Vasha flicked one of his hands between them cutting off his words. "I learned many things sitting in the dark, wet dungeon of Darrius's palace. I learned friendship. I learned how very strong I was capable of being. I learned of the worst in humans and the best. I do not wish to ignore such lessons no matter how hard they were bought."

"Okay then. Where was it Saracan took you next?"

"There was much trade between kingdoms and countries. More than your history scholars know of. We traveled quite extensively even in those days. Saracan had a brother or uncle something like that who served in another kingdom quite a long way away. India was our destination."

"Wow. That's quite a way to travel. How did you get there? Horse back? Camel back?" Wyatt's pencil set ready over the paper, waiting.

"I traveled by palanquin, obviously. That is how all well to do people of the time traveled. The curtains kept my visage a secret and the palanquin kept me in comfort. We traveled with an entourage of Saracan's house. Some twenty to thirty armed men stayed around us at all times. We were quite fortunate. Moreover, the slaves set up camp at night and prepared our food. There were close to fifty of us all told. Quite the spectacle when we passed through the rural villages. The children would follow us asking, '*Who goes there? Is it a King? A Princess*?' All of the armed men would push the children back. Saracan would then hand them a coin and send them on their way.

"It was a long journey. I do not remember how long it took us to get there. Weeks, months, I do not know. I know that when we arrived, Saracan met his uncle or brother," he flapped the irritating memory away with one of his bright blue hands. "Whomever he was, we met him at the city gates. The guardsmen of this city, specifically the men from the palace, wore blue robes tied closed with a yellow and black sash."

"You remember what the guards wore?"

"Yes. It was a beautiful blue. Like the deep parts of the ocean in the evening. Lovely."

"I see."

"I can still hear the sound of the city around the palace. Once again, I was enamored of the lyrical voices shouting their wares or the sound of laughter. Their prayers were lovely… the mantras they chanted echoed in my bones. However, I entered this palace with a bit more suspicion. I did not dare to open the curtains on the palanquin this time. I sat quietly and awaited my fate."

Vasha tossed the green scarf to the side and absently fingered the rings on his fingers. His eyes closed for a moment, head bowed, lost in his memories. When he opened them, he saw a queer look on his friend's face.

"What is it that brings such dark shadows to your lovely eyes, dear Wyatt?" Vasha purred. Wyatt, startled out of his silence, smiled chasing away the shadow of sadness that was there only moments before.

Laughing, he said, "Just thinking about men with dark skin wearing dark blue robes." Vasha's head fell back when he laughed causing the bracelets on his arms to jingle merrily.

"Indeed. I have stories about a few of them. But let us continue," He arranged himself comfortably, folding his four arms across his chest. "They carried my palanquin into the palace and we were followed by many men. I can only assume they were the dark robed men from the city guard but I was not sure. I could sense Saracan close by and that gave me comfort. Of course, it also made me concerned, as he was close by when I was last presented to a King and we know how that turned out."

"Not very well."

"Indeed. I was not taken to a dark room or even a golden room this time. They carried me through the palace and I could feel the air change from indoors to once again being outdoors. The palanquin was set on the ground with care and a heavy silence surrounded me. I waited for someone to tell me what to do. I arranged my hair for the hundredth time. I made sure my lovely necklace was on full display. I wanted to make a good impression, you see." Vasha nodded knowingly as he continued. "After a time, I heard whispers of excitement and that made my heart beat fast. '*The King is coming*' they said."

"I can only imagine how nervous you were, after the last one, I mean."

"Yes. I suppose I was. Due to my youth and suffering from a severe malady of selfishness, however, I was also excited. Once again, my desire to be loved overruled my more recent lessons," his soft laughter was low rumble. "Saracan opened the curtains. I remember seeing how old he really was in the harsh sunlight. His face, once smooth and beautiful, was wrinkled and no longer vibrant. My sadness was short lived because his voice brought me back. '*Smile and be pleasant, my beloved Vashanu. The Emperor awaits you without.*'

So, once again I was brought forth and presented to another Emperor."

"What was he like?" Wyatt asked breathlessly.

Pain and amusement danced in Vasha's smile. "He was as all men of power are—corrupt and cruel. Of course, I did not know this at the time. What I did see was a beautiful garden surrounded by high, brick walls. Flowers bloomed from the most erotic porcelain vases I have ever seen." He leaned close to Wyatt, his yellow eyes alight with mischief. "My favorite was of two men, one as handsome as yourself and the other, a beast with horns. They were locked in a lover's embrace." He reached a blue finger and traced the curve of Wyatt's cheek. "Their bodies were intertwined and the handsome man's face showed pure ecstasy." Slowly, Vasha leaned closer until his lips grazed Wyatt's delicately.

"That sounds…really nice."

"It was," Vasha leaned back to his pillows smiling. Wyatt cleared his throat. "So, the… uh… Emperor."

"Yes. He was there. There were many men and women in attendance in the royal garden, that is where we were, in the Emperor's personal gardens. Saracan bowed low before the Emperor then swept his arms wide announcing me as a messenger of the Gods.

"Of course, I, being an obedient beast, bowed low to my new master. I could feel the eyes of everyone around and hear the sharp intake of breath as they saw me for the first time. The Emperor was a tall man. Thin with pleasantly brown skin. He wore lovely robes of white with silk hems. He liked jewels. I remember that…" Vasha's voice faded as the memories came back. Wyatt waited patiently, turning the pencil in his hand over and over. "Dhana Nanda, that was his name. You must find him in your history books. He was an unpleasant man. Most unpleasant…"

"I'll look him up. Now, I'm not sure of the years here but can you tell me a little about him and the country at the time? What was going on politically?"

Vasha shrugged an elegant shoulder. "I do not know. I saw only the man before me and followed the orders of the Palace Guards. After I was introduced to Dhana, slaves came to pour wine for everyone. Then the slaves passed around little treats made from honey and petite cakes with raisins in them. Those were quite delicious. The wine was not something I enjoyed. It was rather tart, you see. I prefer sweet wines more than the sour ones." He admired a set of ruby rings on one of his hands as he spoke.

"Of course. Sweet wine is good." Wyatt tried to sound interested but he was hungry for details and tapped his pencil on his leg in irritation.

"There was a young child there that day. He was a quite small, chubby little fellow who could barely walk. He was quite taken with me. The women, a group of five who were the Emperor's wives, tried to keep him contained but he insisted on tottering to me and touching my tail. It was amusing to see such a little thing," Vasha leaned forward resting his head between two of his hands. "I had never before seen a small child. I wanted to touch him. He was one of the Princes I later found out."

"It's amazing how children aren't afraid the way adults are."

"Indeed. The little tottering Prince drooled and pulled my tail despite his mother's interruptions. Now, as for the Emperor himself—I did not care for him at all. His eyes were not kind. I saw that right away. I also watched the behavior of those around him. No one looked him in the eyes. Not even the wives. Even the drooling child avoided him it seemed. Therefore, I was right away cautious. I would not allow myself to be a prisoner again. That much I knew. No chains for me."

"Oh good… but I thought—"

"Patience, Wyatt. I told you I had no intention of being a prisoner in chains again and yet, I was this man's prisoner. Confusing, no? It was to me as well. Sometimes, my beloved, one can be a prisoner without chains. It is a different kind of prison. One that keeps you contained but the chains and walls remain invisible."

"If you weren't kept in a dungeon, where did you stay?"

"Oh, as to that… it was a lovely suite of rooms. I was given a servant boy to tend to my needs and an accompaniment of Palace Guards who went everywhere I did. To me, the suite of rooms, walks in the garden, and dining with others were luxuries. I was quite certain I had found the perfect place for me to live out my life in comfort and splendor. You see," Vasha sat upright with excitement. "My suite consisted of a lovely foyer. Two marbled statues greeted me when I arrived and soft Persian rugs covered the marble floors. Flowers were delivered to my rooms daily. In the main sitting room, there was a large couch and everywhere there were overstuffed pillows for my comfort. Like these," he reached out and patted the pillows beneath him. "Soon, my love of gold was well known throughout the palace. Before long, I would receive no less than three gifts from the Emperor a day. I was there perhaps a month or two before I even saw him again. But every day, he would send me gifts."

"I see. He was seducing you."

"Yes, in his way. And as it turns out, I'm quite expensive but can be bought." He chortled looking pleased with himself.

"What was the best gift he gave you then? Which was your favorite?"

"That is a difficult question. Here," he turned from Wyatt, found one of the heavier chests and pulled it closer to them. It was wooden with faded yellow and orange paint that was once obviously quite beautiful before time aged it to the cracked and mangled thing it was now. He opened the lid carefully then turned it to face Wyatt.

Wyatt gasped. "Holy hell!" Vasha watched Wyatt reach out and caress the box. Inside were countless gems of varying colors. Some were tiny, barely large enough to see. Others were as large as an egg. Mixed between the sparkling booty were gold nuggets. Some were carved into the shapes of animals and others decorated with geometric designs. He watched Wyatt feel the cold weight as he lifted a handful of gems closer to his face.

"Beautiful, aren't they? I have collected much over the years. Many and more of these came from my time with the Emperor Dhana Nanda. Payment for my... services."

"Services? What sort of services?"

"There lies the heart of the matter. Let me explain," Vasha sat back and reached for his long wooden pipe. He stuffed it with a dark tobacco as he spoke. "After a few months I was summoned to the Emperor's private chambers. I remember feeling excited and rather proud of myself, you see. I thought I was undeniably lucky to have fallen into such a splendiferous situation. When the guards summoned me, I made certain I was suitable for an audience with the Emperor and followed them to two large, golden doors."

"Ooh. Your favorite." Wyatt snickered.

"Just so. When I arrived, I entered a whole new world. Everywhere I looked there were naked men and women. Their skin dyed the most preposterous colors. When I entered, two women whose skin was as green as grass, knelt on either side of the doors. Feathers from a peacock hung from their heads. Small colorful jewels sparkled from their breasts. The guards closed the doors behind me and the women crawled on the floor before me, beckoning me to follow."

"Well that's odd."

"I thought so as well. However, the women were beautiful, so it escaped me the absurdity of it all. Dhana's rooms were cavernous. As I followed the crawling beauties, we passed small enclaves where, I thought, stood beautiful sculptures. It was not until the third or fourth one we passed did I realize they were living people! Can you believe such a thing?"

"I've heard of living art before. People do it even now."

"Do they? I must see this one day," he brought the smoking pipe to his mouth and took several puffs, releasing a cloud of dark smoke into the air. "I thought it was all magnificent. At the end of the long room was a pool where young maidens frolicked. They were quite young. I did not know it at the time but these were young girls Dhana spotted about the city and took them for his own."

"What do you mean took them for his own? He'd raise random kids he saw?"

Vasha smirked. "No, dear one. Not just raise them. He would feed them, for many in the cities were poor. He would give them beautiful clothes and gifts. Then, he would take them as his concubines."

"Oh."

"Dhana greeted me like an old friend. '*Come to me, Vashanu.*' He said. He was nude with several painted women draped over him. I approached the Emperor and was immediately surrounded by men and women. I had never been so close to a nude man or woman and I found that I liked it very much."

"Which one?" Wyatt smirked lifting his eyebrow.

"Both. The men were muscular. One in particular had skin died such a dark blue he looked almost purple. It was lovely. He greeted me with a kiss. Then the young woman painted silver approached me. Her black hair was an amazing contrast to the silver on her skin. I remember her for a number of reasons, first because she had a large emerald embedded in her navel, I liked that. Second, she was not shy about touching me. Her hands, those small delicate hands gently touched the most secret parts of me. I was immediately aroused, as you can imagine."

Wyatt made a production about fanning himself. "Whew."

"Yes, I can still remember the feeling of her mouth gently sliding over my rather excited manhood. That was a completely new experience for me. Dhana watched and directed the man painted blue to mount me. Another thing I had never experienced before. I found I could not keep still, as you can imagine. With the little silver minx pleasuring me, and the blue man taking his pleasure, I reached out for the nearest person I could find. Dhana nodded, seeming quite interested in what I was doing. The young woman I grabbed was a small thing. Her skin was red and so soft. She smelled of spices and sweat. She did not fight me as I touched her. I was free for a few moments to explore her perky breasts and what lay between her thighs. She seemed to enjoy it, as did the Emperor. I could not keep that up for long for I was quite innocent. I experienced my first *petite morte*, as the French say."

"That's a hell of a first time."

Vasha nodded enthusiastically. "It was indeed. I remember collapsing to the floor as the man finished himself and I was completely won over. Not only was I surrounded by riches and beauty but the pleasure I had always craved was finally at my fingertips."

"Seems like the Emperor liked a lot of things you did. You guys had a lot in common?"

A dark look passed over Vasha's face. "For a time, yes. You see, we passed many days like that one. Day after day, I was summoned to his private chambers and partook in the most glorious of sexual acts. One day it was only men and I learned how to please a man in many ways. I am quite large but they did not seem to mind it when I mounted them. The women were more forgiving of my size. I would play a game Dhana enjoyed very much. He wanted to see how many women I could pleasure at the same time. My record was seven."

"Seven? At once?"

A look of pride and a flirtatious flick of his hair made Wyatt laugh. "I am quite good at giving pleasure."

"Sounds like it. Here I thought I knew some freaks in my day."

"A freak? I do not understand this?"

"It's a slang term for someone who is… ah… interesting in the boudoir."

"Oh, then I am most definitely a freak." Vasha concluded with a small smile.

"I know you enjoyed yourself, I mean, how could you not? But did things go bad? What happened?"

"Did things go bad?" he parroted with a strange expression. "You could say that," Vasha took a few more puffs from the long pipe then set it gently down beside him. "One evening the Palace Guards came to get me. It was much later in the day than I was accustomed. I was gifted a vat of wine that was surprisingly good and had been imbibing all afternoon. So, I was quite intoxicated when the guards took me from my rooms. We did not, as was custom, go to the Emperor's suite of rooms. Instead, we travelled deep into the bowels of the Palace. It was not dark and dirty as my previous enclosure. Intricately painted tapestries hung from the ceiling concealing the drab walls and torches lighting our way. Somewhere deep within me, I was frightened. However, no one had ever hurt me before in Dhana's Palace. So, I followed.

"We came to two large wooden doors. Carved into the wood were the most amazing reliefs of the pornographic sort. I was not able to study them, that time, before I was ushered into the room. As the door closed behind me, the hollow room became clear. Are you certain you wish to hear the rest, young Wyatt? It is not pleasant."

"I'm certain. Go on." Wyatt tried to put on a brave face, encouraging Vasha to continue.

"Very well," Vasha exhaled and settled back against a large purple pillow. "I was met by the painted peacock girls that served the Emperor. They beckoned me to follow and I did. As we walked, their skin slapped the stone floor. I was so transfixed, watching their buttocks move as they crawled, I almost missed the scene in which I entered." He cleared his throat and continued. "There was a man lying on the ground. His hands and feet were bound in a way that his legs were uncomfortably spread wide. His arms were tied tight above his head. His face was pure agony. I did not understand until we walked closer. There was a large wooden phallus inside him." Vasha held up two hands and made a circle about the size of a baseball. "About this large around. Most uncomfortable."

"Damn. Why?"

"In good time. Let me continue," Wyatt apologized and Vasha reached for a green scarf and began twirling it around his fingers. "I was as curious as you are now. Why was this man bound and forced to endure such brutality? Continuing on, we passed a young woman who hung from her ankles, legs spread wide apart, her womanhood open for all to see. Except there was something quite wrong with this woman. She hung as limp as a fish. I do not know what was done to her. I do believe she was dead as she hung there although I cannot be sure.

"Further down there were many young men and women bound, gagged, bleeding, and all of them in such terrible pain. I wondered, had I done something wrong? Would I be bound and hurt as these young people were? The effects of the wine were quickly wearing off as we approached the Emperor. He stood with a familiar looking whip in his hand. I knew what that whip would do to my skin so I hesitated to approach him further. '*Come closer, Vashanu*' he said to me. I did not want to. But I did not want to anger him either. From the floor, I heard a woman sobbing. '*Please...please help us.*' She sobbed. The Emperor beckoned me once again and I obeyed. He smiled as I approached him and he handed me the whip. I remember feeling the weight of the leather in my hands. I felt the weight of the straps that had metal teeth tied at the ends."

"Oh no…"

"Oh yes. My eye searched the darkness and I saw many, many people in the dark room. The painted slaves were all on their hands and knees, heads down, and perpetually silent. '*Come, Vashanu, let us discipline these naughty children.*' He said to me. I was still confused, perhaps the change of scenery and perhaps from the wine but I searched his face for answers. He laughed at me and snatched the whip from my hands. With expertise, he cracked the whip and it struck its mark. I hadn't noticed the man there at all. He was tied to a large pillar and he was most certainly on his way to the afterlife. Strips of his skin hung in tatters. Even from his scalp. I could see the white of his skull in the dimly lit room. Of course, there was blood. I did not smell it at first, you see, because the small torches were also burning incense. It was quite overwhelming."

"The smell or the scenery?"

"Both. Dhana laughed at the bleeding man and waved his hands for the slaves to take him away. From the corners, slaves painted black untied the dying man from the pillar and took him away. These black painted slaves were different, you see. They did not have the duties the others did. These slaves lived in the dungeons. They ate, slept, and cleaned up behind the Emperor's activities."

"This is so strange. I've never heard of this before."

"Well, the custom exists still, I assure you. I will explain it all in time. Let me tell you the worst of it first."

"Sorry. Go ahead."

"The slaves who were painted black were called Shadows. They were not people to him, you see. They were only shadows of people painted black so they might blend into the darkness of the dungeon. Dhana did not consider any of his slaves as people actually so this is not unique. The color of their skin meant they were concealed from sight but always there. I learned of the color hierarchy as the years passed. However, almost everyone feared the Shadows. They did not speak as none of the Shadows had tongues. They had their own language with hand signals and grunts that none but themselves understood.

"Before I knew what was happening, another person was hung from the ropes on the pillar. She was a young woman, perhaps twenty. She was crying and kept pleading with Dhana to release her. I asked him, *'What did this girl do?'* His face contorted into a terrible scowl. He approached the woman, grabbed a fistful of her hair and pulled it to the side. It caused her to cry out and more tears fell down her cheeks. I wanted to help this young woman. She was nude, tied to a pillar at the mercy of an angry Emperor. It did not bode well for her. *'You dare deny me?'* Dhana was screaming into her ear. I remember, I glanced back at the painted slaves and none so much as flinched. They knelt on the floor like well behaved, colorful dogs."

"Was he some sort of sadist or something?"

"Something like that. That young woman caught his eye in court. He wanted her body and she refused him. You see, the Shadows were also tasked to acquire the occupants in the dungeon. They would slip out into the night and return with their prey. They would strip them and tie their hands until the Emperor came to dispense his unique form of justice."

"What happened to her?"

"The Emperor had his way with her. He took her there as she screamed and cried. He did not want her dead so she was not whipped. Instead, he kept her as his pet."

"His pet?"

"Yes. Dhana had many pets. They were chained and brutally beaten for some slight or another. Others were kept in better conditions but we were still his pets."

"We?"

"Have you not figured it out yet, young Wyatt? I was his pet. No different to him than his painted slaves, the Shadows, or the poor souls he tortured in that cavernous room. The only difference was that a part of my duties as his pet... was to be his instrument of revenge."

"What do you mean?"

"What I mean is, he would do the raping and I would do the killing."

"Oh. That's... that's awful."

"It was. He kept the young girl for a few weeks before I was instructed to kill her. The Shadows handed me a long blade and mimicked slicing her throat with their fingers. I was distraught but knew I must do as I was told or else," Vasha coughed a bit. "Or else I would no longer have the life I had become accustomed to."

The shed was quiet. Vasha watched Wyatt wrestle with what he just heard. "So, you killed her?" he finally asked.

Vasha nodded. "I did. I told myself it was a mercy at the time. One clean cut with the blade and she fell to the floor as dead as one can be. The Shadows removed her body and took it to her family so they would dispose of it. I find that the most cruel part, if you ask me."

"Among other things."

"I know it is hard to hear, this part of my history. I assure you it does end."

"I know. It's just… I don't know. I have a hard time thinking of you as… as… the villain."

"Was I a villain? Or was I a slave? The question is one for philosophers. I did what needed to be done in order to survive."

"Wait a minute," Wyatt held up his hand. "You are capable of ripping apart people with little effort. You're faster than even Decker. You could have made different choices here, let's be real."

"Indeed, let us be real," Vasha leaned forward with a frown. "I had nowhere to go. I was ill-equipped to live on my own safely. The reality is, dear Wyatt, that I was forced to choose between a life of running for my life and hiding or living amongst beauty and riches. I chose what my heart and soul needed at the time."

They stared at one another for a long time in silence before Wyatt smiled and ran a hand through his wavy locks. "I'm sorry, Vasha. I was just a little shocked. I apologize."

"No apology necessary. It was a brutal time and I was a part of Dhana's brutality. There is no denying that. We all played a part in his demented exploits. The painted slaves, the Shadows, and me. We did as we were told or else we would suffer the way the captive pets in the dungeon did."

"I understand. I really do. Let's keep going." Wyatt tried to smile but it didn't reach his eyes.

"There were many women kept as Dhana's pets. He preferred beating the women and raping them before bringing me in. One particular man was a man of politics who was famous for speaking out against the Emperor. The Shadows caught him out one night and he was promptly displayed for the Emperor's amusement. This particular man was a brave soul. He cursed and spat at the Emperor and called him a monster. He was quite right but he certainly paid for that bit of honesty. Even when whipped, the man cursed the entire Nanda family. He cursed his children and cursed the Gods. Dhana thought this all very frustrating so he called me forward. The angry man was shocked and terrified after setting eyes upon me. I finished my cup of wine and approached the Emperor. I asked him what he required of me. With an evil smile, he said he wanted me to pleasure the man. He demanded I make him enjoy it or I would pay the price.

"All of this he thought was good fun. He settled back on pillows, surrounded by his painted slaves and waited for me to pleasure the angry man."

"That's a tall order."

"It was. I tried being gentle with the man. He fought and continued to curse Dhana even as I took my pleasure of him. I whispered for him to be quiet. I tried to sooth him with kind words but he managed to bring his head back and smacked me right on my perfectly lined nose."

"Uh oh."

"I was quite angry about that. I had, so far, avoided any type of bodily harm since coming to this palace and refused to accept defeat. So, I took the man harder. His cries of outrage became cries of pain. Once I felt the fight leave him, I turned my attention to pleasuring him. He did not want it but the body will not fight for long and I managed to break him. He wept when his climax was over. Bleeding and spent, I returned to the Emperor's side."

"Damn, Vasha. How long did this go on? I mean, how many did you-"

"Kill? I killed many pets over a number of years. It was distasteful, yes, but I continued to tell myself it was a mercy. Once someone was taken by the Shadows into the dungeons, they only left wrapped in a rug dead by my hand. It was a dark time for me. I drank too much. I ate rich foods and took my pleasure with the painted slaves and pets alike. Nevertheless, it was not as satisfying for me as you might think. The sexual pleasure made me content for a time but it was always short lived."

"I get it. There wasn't any real connection with anyone."

"Precisely. There were times the Emperor whipped me. However, they never lasted long and I was almost always immediately forgiven. If I failed to break one of pets or hesitated in taking someone, he would whip me. I began to resent the man. It took a good long while for the riches and the magnificent surroundings to no longer amuse me. I became greedy. I wanted to leave the palace but I would not leave empty handed nor as anyone's prisoner."

"What made you start to see things that way?"

"Saracan's death. He was an old man when he died. He did know who he was or where he was. A terrible thing, growing old. I was not with him when he died but once he left this world, I felt so terribly alone. He did try, my Saracan, to save me from the evils of his time. He was a good man." Vasha blinked a few times and Wyatt looked away respectfully. "Once he died and I made my decision to leave, everything changed around me."

"What do you mean? Did they know what you were planning?"

"No. There was much upheaval in the cities. I learned this from my little servant boy. He told me, in hushed tones late at night, about the meetings in the city of rich families who wished to overthrow Dhana. There was much subterfuge and political games surrounding me. I do not have the head for such matters so I cannot explain the details. All I know is that the wealthy families, many of whom lost a family member or two to Dhana's Shadows, were meeting and creating alliances. This obviously disturbed Dhana greatly."

"I'm sure it did. Did they do it? Was he overthrown?"

"You are a terribly impatient young man. I am coming to that part," Vasha chided with a smile. "Now, I must tell you what I was up to while those smarter than I plotted with one another." He leaned in and whispered in a conspiratorial tone. "I was stealing from the Emperor."

"Oh well, that was dangerous."

"It is the truth. I gathered all of my gifts from him in a secret place. It was enough to all fit in one chest. That would not do. I made it my mission to acquire as much gold as I could on any given day. Jewels, necklaces, rings, coins by the bag full… all of it I spirited away to my rooms. I was in cahoots with my servant boy. He loved me, you see. I treated him well and never beat him. I fed him from my plate when he was hungry and called the healers when he was ill. His name was Dipankar. A chubby boy with bright eyes."

"That's an unusual name."

"It means One Who Lights Lamps. Not very original, if I may say so. Many of the slaves in the palace were families. They were bred there and their children then served. Many for multiple generations. So it was with Dipankar and why he knew so much. The slaves saw and heard everything. I had my suspicions that the painted slaves whispered secrets to the palace slaves and kitchen slaves. Many, if not all, knew of the boiling unrest and inevitable revolution in the city. I cared only for fleeing the palace with my bountiful wealth. I also knew I could not manage such a thing on my own. So, I convinced young Dipankar that he and his family should come away with me."

"Oh, now that's the Vasha I know and love!"

"He was quite keen on the idea of all of the scheming we were doing. He would giggle and clap his hands when I showed him the loot I absconded with for the day. A few times, Dipankar added to our growing stash. Here, let me show you," and from another smaller chest, Vasha pulled out a brown leather bag. "It is not the original bag as that one has long since fallen apart with time. But here, I will show you a few of the trinkets young Dipankar found for our wild escape." He held the brown bag in one hand while another dug inside. A slight frown flickered across his face until he found what he was looking for.

With a flourish, he placed a small ivory elephant in Watt's hands. It was no bigger than his palm but felt heavy. The elephant's feet were dipped in gold and the eyes reflected flecks of emeralds.

"This is gorgeous. You kept this for this long?" he asked handing the priceless statue back to Vasha's care.

"Yes. Little Dipankar was very proud of this bit of thievery. He stole it from one of the Prince's chambers. I never had need to sell it and I like it. It reminds me of him." Vasha placed the elephant back into the bag and closed the string shut tightly. "Now, to the important parts. There was a man," Vasha spoke as he placed his beloved memories back inside the chest. "A man whom everyone in the cities rallied behind. His name was Chandragupta Maurya."

"That's a hell of a name."

"Yes. He was an important man. A wealthy one and powerful at that. What was most important though was that he brought hope to the people. He had plans to trade with other empires and all sorts of nonsense that I do not understand. His nonsense, however, made everyone hopeful and excited. Whispering slaves brought tales of meetings with this merchant and that trader with such and such powerful family. The emperor in the meantime was at a turning point of his own."

"Did he hear all of these whispers too? Did he know this other guy was after his throne?"

"Oh yes. He tried, several times, to send the Shadows out and bring the traitors to him but the Shadows either failed or were paid to fail. I never knew the truth of it."

"That's interesting. I wonder what really happened?"

Vasha shrugged and reached for his pipe. "I tend to think they were paid to fail in their mission. In doing so, they also knew they were courting the Emperor's wrath. I am not entirely sure of the truth but there you have it. What I do know is that Dhana was losing all self-control. He would kill his pets himself, screaming about treachery and lies. The painted slaves were more terrified than normal. I felt the water boiling to the top of the kettle, as they say. Something terrible was about to happen and I wanted out of the palace."

"Sure. Did you have a plan?"

"I had a sort of plan. However, plans never seem to work out quite the way we want them to, do they?"

"Nope." Wyatt laughed.

"Well, here I was," he took a puff from his pipe and seeing it was not lit, he brought a match to the tip and puffed a few times to make it catch. "Here I was with all of this fortune but I needed to get myself and Dipankar's family out as well. We decided to enlist the help of another member of Dipankar's family who worked in the royal kitchens. They would smuggle us all out in the dead of night and we would be fast away before anyone knew we were gone. But,"

"But it didn't work out that way?" Wyatt asked with a pained expression.

"It did not and I will tell you why. Dhana had the terrible idea that because he did not know who was loyal to him in the palace and who was not, he would execute us all."

"Us? As in you too?"

"As in me too. Such a terrible shock really, to hear someone planning your death right where you could hear them and him pretending we could not understand! It was as if we really were nothing but animals to him. He spoke about us the way one would speak about a dog who does not know better," he growled. "Forgive me. The memory still causes much grief."

"Understandable."

"I thank you. So, the night he decided he wanted us all to die, we were summoned to his private chambers. Little did I know that he had most of his pets in the dungeon put to the knife already. He and his Shadows did the deeds before summoning the rest of us. When he arrived in his rooms, he was wild eyed and ranting. His body was covered in blood. It made a frightening sight because the Shadows trailed into his chambers behind him terrifying everyone. He started to give orders for the Shadows to kill his house slaves first—this included my Dipankar. I could not have that. Much less, the deaths of the painted slaves with whom I had shared many pleasures. They were as helpless as baby kittens and everyone tried to remain composed but I could smell the fear rolling off all of them. That mixed with the old scent of sex was heady. I remember approaching the Emperor and slowly taking the blade from his hands. He looked so surprised," Vasha's laugh was a mixture of hilarity and menace. "I took the blade and he turned to look at me with such an expression of confusion that I smiled. Everyone around us froze. I told him that he would kill no more innocents. I gave him a choice, to leave the palace or to die right there."

"And?"

"And he lifted his chin, placed his hands on his hips, and told the Shadows to kill me. His demand was met with understandable silence. No one moved. I believe they feared me. Most do, you know."

"Until they get to know you. Then we love you."

"I do not think they loved me but they were thankful when I gave Dhana the mercy I had given many others in his name. I cut his royal throat and watched as he died with the arrogant expression of defiance still on his face until the bitter end."

"Whew… so you killed him. Then what happened?"

"Complete and utter chaos." They both laughed. "The slaves cried and the Shadows looked lost. They knew they could not easily escape notice because of their painted skin. I managed to calm many down and invited them to leave with me and Dipankar's family, who had successfully avoided the threat of slaughter by hiding in the ovens. We left the palace that very night. Dipankar, his family, about seven painted slaves, a few of the Shadows, and myself. We left in silence carrying our worldly possessions and a little food spirited away from the kitchens. We wrapped the painted slaves in robes and shawls to cover them. That is how I left the service of the last Emperor of the Nanda Dynasty. That is also the night that the Maurya Empire began."

"Wow. You like, brought down entire Empires." Wyatt said in awe.

"Perhaps it would have happened without my involvement," Vasha fingered the gold bracelets on his wrists. "Who knows? But we came away from the palace and made a home for ourselves in a lovely house by a river just outside of the city."

"All of you together? Seems crowded."

"Much like our current situation," He reached for a goblet of extraordinary beauty filling it with wine. "Here, taste this. It has only aged a few decades but it is sweet." Handing Wyatt the heavy goblet, Vasha reached for another and filled that one as well. The sweet aroma filled the air.

"What flavor of wine is this?"

"Fig wine. One of my favorites. I do so like figs." He took a deep drink from his glass and refilled it once more. "The time immediately following our exit from the Emperor's service was fairly uneventful. The Kingdom flourished under the new empire of the Maurya family."

"And all of you? Did the slaves take to being free and colorless well?"

Vasha chuckled. "It took them quite some time to learn to be free. Many of them looked to me as their new Master once we were settled. No decision was made without my approval. From where we slept to what we bought for food, the slaves—former slaves—still required guidance from someone. Perhaps that is a normal thing? Going from slave to free cannot be an easy transition. How does one do it?" he seemed to be asking the spirits of the long dead instead of Wyatt. "How does one go from being an object, something bought and sold as if cattle to having full power of themselves? It must have been bewildering." He placed the cup down and folded both sets of hands across his chest. "The Shadows suffered the most. I do not remember how many initially left the palace with us but I remember one simply disappeared one night never to be heard from again. Another took his own life by plunging a dagger in his stomach and died a slow death. Quite the mess and it upset many of the slaves—former slaves." He corrected himself.

"I'd imagine. Why'd he do it? Why'd he kill himself?"

"Perhaps," Vasha sighed heavily then continued. "Perhaps the weight of our deeds in the dungeon were too much for him to bear. Perhaps the paint on his skin and the blood on his hands defined his existence. Whatever the reason, he left this world alone and afraid. I did not want my Dipankar to suffer so. My little one was ever so committed to my wellbeing. In truth, that little fellow ran the house. He was a master of his own making. He made sure our coffers were full. He dictated the duties of all who lived in the house, quite impressive for a child of his few years. Alas, like all things, this arrangement too ended."

"Badly?"

"Is there any other way anything ends?"

"I'm sorry."

"We lived together, our malformed family of former slaves and murderers quite happily. The new empire opened trade routes with the rest of the world in short order. Little Dipankar dreamed of the large boats anchored offshore. I never saw them but he spoke of them so often I felt as if I needn't bother to make the trip because he described them so well." His voice trailed off as his face changed from laughter to melancholy. "A few years went by and one by one my little freed slaves left our home. Some saved enough coin to make their own way. A couple married and started their own families. Dipankar grew up and his dreams of sailing the seas on his glorious ships finally became too much for him. His love for me diminished under the weight of the call of the sea. My little Dipankar, barely a man, left me with kisses and promises of his return for the adventures on the boats he loved so much." Vasha stretched and began the laborious effort to stand in his cramped home. "I feel this is an opportune time to halt our story. After all, I was no longer a prisoner and all was well for me then."

Wyatt stood and began to gather his things, taking a quick swig to drain the wine from his glass. "Vasha, did you ever see Dipankar again? Did he come back?"

Vasha opened the doors to the shed. With eyes closed, he breathed in the brisk air. "No. He perished on the ship that carried him away from me. He was lost at sea." He did not wait for Wyatt's reply but slipped out of the shed into the open air. He knew what it would be. Attempts to balm an old wound were wasted, he thought. It was done and Dipankar was long dead at the bottom of the sea. Did he ever mourn the little fellow's passing? He could not remember. He could remember what came next and he did not want to start that part of his story yet. He needed fresh air and to stretch his legs. He needed to remember he was no longer chained. He needed to remember that he was loved.

"Brother," Theo's voice whispered from behind him. A small smile played on Vasha's painted lips. How comforting his brothers were to him now, he mused. With a single thought of longing his brother came to provide him with what he needed most. "Are you well?"

"Yes. I am well." He turned to welcome his brother into his embrace. Theo was the only other one of them that craved the physical love of another. Theo curled under his arm and wrapped his body as close to his as possible. "And you, brother, are you well?" They began to walk together with no real destination in mind.

Theo paused before answering. "Yes. I am well but…" he turned his head up to meet his brother's eyes. His love was mirrored in the yellow cat eyes they shared. "Mela has asked some troublesome questions of late."

"What sorts of things is our little witch asking about and why do they trouble you? Wyatt has asked me many questions and I tell him everything."

"Are you telling him your story as Decker did?" Vasha nodded. "That is good. It is good to share our stories so that we may understand one another. We gain healing from the telling."

"Yes. But let us go back to your concerns over our little witch. What did she ask you?"

"Well, she has been showing an unhealthy curiosity for Azul." A heavy weight landed in Vasha's chest at the mention of his brother's name. "I do not tell you this to cause you pain, brother. I know well your… disfavor for our eldest brother. What I was not aware of was Mela's depth of interest in him. She asks me many questions about what he looks like, what his abilities are, and even asked how Decker and I found him."

Vasha stopped walking and frowned. "Why does she wish to know these things? Did she tell you?"

Theo shook his head. "No, but I can feel her intent. She is curious and wishes to prepare to protect us should it be necessary. Vashanu," Theo pleaded in words and expression. "Please help me to dissuade her of anymore questions about him. The more we speak of him, the more we say his name—"

"The easier he will be able to find us, yes. I shall have words with her. Thank you for telling me and I share your concerns. It would not be a glorious reunion should he find where we are. Not with all of the other intruders recently."

"No. Not good at all. Vasha…"

"I know, my innocent one. I know you miss him." He pulled his brother closer and they continued to walk until the house was out of sight.

Chapter Three

"**S**on of a bitch!" Mela cried as Vasha once more knocked her to the ground.

"You are getting cocky, little witch. Your magicks are only good if you are alive and conscious to cast a spell." She pushed herself up onto her hands and knees, sweat dripped from the tip of nose as she gained her composure.

"I can't block all four of your swords." She whined.

"That much is clear. All I am asking of you is to try." He laughed as she mumbled some particularly colorful promises that included where she would try to put her practice sword. "I tire and require a drink. Do you care to join me?" She didn't answer right away but silently followed him to the impromptu meeting place beside the back porch. Mela tossed the wooden practice swords on the ground and gracelessly plopped down to the dirt and began to bite her nails.

He wasn't truly thirsty, merely looking for an opportunity to broach the subject of his damned elder brother. "My dear, might I have a word with you?"

"Mmhmm."

"Theo tells me you are more than a little curious about our eldest brother. Why is this?"

She rolled on her side to face him. "He's a danger to all of us. Look what he did to Decker," she pointed an accusing finger to Decker's empty seat on the porch. "Then there's Theo who not only got hurt but he was so sad. If Azul comes here—"

"I apologize to interrupt but you need to stop this immediately. What you do not understand is that our brother is as pure a magical creature as one could be. He is the things the legends of dragons are made of. He possesses abilities that far exceed all of ours, with you as the exception of course."

"Then I should be the one—"

"No! You, little one, need to focus on the threats that are already standing on our borders. We do not need to invite yet another deadly encounter here. Erase him from your mind. Stop all of this talk about him and for the love of all the Gods stop having Theo talk about him. One can forge a connection with our eldest brother, born of want and knowledge of him. The more you know of him, the more you force Theo—or any of us—to speak of him, you invite a connection to him we will be unable to sever. He would be able to swoop from the skies, land on your doorstep, and in his wake, he will destroy us all. He has all but said so. Do you understand, Mela? This is of the greatest importance." He waited, watching her brown eyes search his face for the truth in his words. He hoped she believed him and took his words to heart. No one, least of all her, had the faintest idea of how deadly his eldest brother could be. Finally, after moment, Mela nodded and agreed.

"All right. I didn't know that. I just—we just wanted to be thorough. I don't want any more surprises."

"I do understand and I think your efforts valiant. However, in this case, I beg of you to trust in me and what I know. He is a lost cause. He is dangerous. To court him is to court all of our deaths. Leave him to his misery and let us live."

She nodded. "All right."

"Everyone looks to you for guidance, make sure you share my warnings with the other witches." She nodded again. The small crease between her eyes deepened with her frown. "I am to wash and rest. I believe young Wyatt will be coming to see me tonight."

"Yeah, he'll be here after Annabelle comes home from school. He's super nervous."

"Then he is a good father. Rest but do not forget to stretch. Decker will no doubt wish to train this evening in his way."

She groaned but did as he suggested. As she stood to reach her arms over her head, he turned away with a smile. She was a lovely girl who cared for all of them deeply. Her depth of love was also a weakness. Any enemy of value would see this and exploit it at the earliest opportunity. He must remember to discuss this with Decker the next they spoke.

***

"I'm here! I'm here! I didn't forget." Wyatt rushed into the shed as if on wings carrying with him the smells of wood on a fire and musky aftershave. Vasha smiled and welcomed him inside with a glass of fig wine.

"Sit. Catch your breath."

"Thank you," he took a deep drink and closed his eyes. "Perfect."

"How did the day go? Did little Annabelle do well on her first day of school?"

"Surprisingly good actually. Until she let the teacher know that her dead grandmother wants her to get married and have babies. I had to have a talk with her about that sort of thing." Their laughter echoed in the small space. "Overall, it was good for her. She played with another little girl at recess. I was so floored when she told me she hadn't been on a slide before. Her teacher said at recess that's all she did, go up and down the slide with her new friend. I forget sometimes the kind of sheltered life she lived before."

"This is good. A normal environment will help her adjust and, in enough time, she will act like any other little girl her age."

"That's what I hope for her. I mean, she's not like other little girls, is she? She'll never have a normal life."

"Certainly, a heavy weight on such small shoulders. It is lucky for her you are there to hold her up. I shudder to think of where she would be now had you not taken her in."

"Thank you," he smiled seemingly pleased with the world. "I have my notes somewhere," he dug around in his leather satchel and produced the small notebook overflowing with lose papers and a pencil. "Ah ha. Here we are." He flipped through the pages until he found the page that was half-full of small, neat handwriting.

"We left off when I lived in the house by the river. I have thought long about what came next. My memory is not as detailed as my brother's but I have done my best to remember the events and what came next. The next chapter should interest you as this was when I was introduced to another way of life and the magical arts. Many of the things I know now are due to those who taught me during this time. It might be best if I explained what happened to bring me there first before I go any further with that subject.

"You see, I once again found myself alone except for a few aging former slaves and a large house that held more echoes than life. I was becoming bored and anxious for I knew that when the old women died, I would be completely alone once more. These women knew this and planned for my care after their death. For many months, they were meeting with amiable souls in the marketplace to discuss my future. Until last night, I never gave much thought on the subject. However, now it gives me pause over how much of my life depended on the good nature of others." He delicately shook his head and continued. "The old women came to me one night with strangers in tow.

These strangers were women wearing garbs of the highest quality silks. One was a lovely shade of pink lined with flowers embroidered in gold thread. It was divine."

Wyatt attempted to bring the conversation away from the woman's clothes and back to the story. "What did they say?"

"Say? I don't remember what they said in detail. Only that they wished to take me away to the house of their master, a Sultan." He said the last word with great emphasis. "I was weary, of course, to be beneath the heel of yet another master. The women assured me that I would lead the most elegant life in the Sultan's palace and I would want for nothing. I was promised safety. Most importantly, the women promised I would never feel the end of the lash on my flesh again. They pledged their lives to that promise."

"You went with them then? Seems too sweet of a deal to pass up if I were you."

"Yes. It was… sweet. In less than a fortnight, I travelled with my new friends away from my humble home by the river. I gifted that to the old women as I recall." He shifted his position so he could rummage through a box that sat beside him. "The travelling was not hard. He went slowly in covered wagons. These were elaborate wagons, you understand. They were made of painted wood and lined with cushions in order to make travelling quite comfortable. Steeds with the most lovely, flowing manes pulled them. I did admire these creatures with their regal ways. To find such haughtiness in a horse of all things!" he laughed deeply.

"Imagine that." Wyatt laughed with him.

"We only travelled at night, you see. I believe that was in part so that I could watch the countryside change without anyone seeing us. The further away from what I knew brought scenery quite foreign to me. Oh Wyatt," he sat back with a dreamy expression. "If only the world were different so that you and I could travel to these places and behold their wonders together. Such beauty now must hide beneath the shadows of war. It is a sad thing. The world you live in now will never know the exquisiteness of those times. Change is not always good, my friend."

"All we have left are pictures really. Even the artifacts historians find are stored away and some are even destroyed."

"A travesty indeed. I have done my best to save mementos for this very reason, you see. It helps me to remember, yes, but I am able to preserve the beauty and artistry myself. One day, perhaps when I finally leave this world, I will leave my legacy to proper historians who will show my little treasures. Perhaps it will inspire the world to be a beautiful place once more. Who knows?" his voice drifted off as he continued his digging in the box beside him. "The ladies who travelled with me were of the Sultan's court. I do not remember their names though. In truth, they kept their distance during our travels. I do not know why and at the time, I did not much care. I was off on another adventure, you understand. They saw to my needs each day they left me to the comfort of my wagon. I watched the world change each evening as we set off for the Sultan's court. Weeks, perhaps a month passed before we entered the land ruled by the Sultan. You see, in those times, a Sultan ruled much like a Lord ruled in Europe. Each of their courts were as unique offering both beauty and learning to its people. It was an amazing time.

"When we reached the Sultan's palace it was a wondrous sight to behold. Granted, it was night when we arrived but the many lanterns lit the streets so could still see much as we travelled.

"The expansive home we arrived to was white decorated with colorful tiles and statues in the gardens. It was a lovely sight even at night. Another group of women, this one large and containing women of various ages, greeted the old women in the shadows. Before long, I shuffled from the wagon and was presented to the group of women so they could get a better look. What was most curious about this night, I remember, was they were not afraid of me. Can you imagine that? They looked me over as if I were a prized horse to be bought at auction."

"Every man's deepest desire. A stud for hire."

"Do you think? An odd desire to be sure if that is so. I felt rather odd if truth be told. However, I grew accustomed to the feeling before long. Before I knew what was happening or had any opportunity to decide what I would do, the women urged me with soft words and gentle nudges into a wing of the great manse I found myself. It felt airy, many open windows and archways open to the night sky. I smelled the city, the desert, and the people who were near. It was a pleasant place from what I remember of it.

"This group of women followed me into an indoor water garden. It was night but there were candles and torches lit everywhere. There was an oasis right there inside of the manse. It was spectacular. It was quite common in those days for people of means to keep gardens to show their wealth. Much like a large house or many heads of cattle."

"Now they just buy ridiculously expensive cars and overpriced clothing."

"Yes! That is what I have noticed as well. Not as exciting though, is it? I prefer an expansive water garden and a fine wine to loud, ugly motor cars."

"I think I agree with you. We've changed a lot haven't we? People I mean…"

"Oh yes… and no. The love of beauty has certainly diminished over time though. Instead of trying to build beautiful things that will last forever, people want themselves to be beautiful. This is folly, you see, because the beauty humans try to preserve can never last. Their efforts are in vain and the beauty fades with their last breath. This leaves the world uglier than it was before and void of any new beauty. Gone are the times when artists are thought to be important members of a society. Gone are the days when building a cathedral or a statue earns one's name in the history books. Now… madness and vanity rule." Vasha poured more wine and sipped from his goblet. He watched the small frown play across Wyatt's face and wondered if he had insulted him. Perhaps. But he would not take his words back because they were true.

"What did you do in the gardens? Was it the Sultan's home you were in?" Wyatt still frowned but did not address the thoughts Vasha knew bothered him.

"Yes. It was one of the Sultan's many homes. The one I found myself in was aptly named Sparkling Halls. The water from the gardens was maneuvered somehow throughout the massive home to create small waterfalls and sparkling pools in almost every room. It was a wonder to be sure. There in Sparkling Halls, I was fed marvelous meals and had my very first massage. A thing even a beast can enjoy."

"Your first massage. That's interesting. I guess I never thought about it but I suppose that would be something you would enjoy, eh?"

"Beyond a doubt," he flicked at a speck of dirt on his pillow. "What is important at this moment in the story is why I was there. Even more important were the old women. You see, they brought me to live at this Manse for a reason. The Sultan had need of me for a reason. The Sultan had a Harem of women whose sole purpose was to pleasure him. Imagine that? His wives were present in the Manse as well but their purpose was to give him sons and raise his children. I was to have no contact with the Sultan's family, that rule was made clear to me by a tiny woman who had lived far beyond her required years. She walked in a half-bent posture and spent most of the time talking to ghosts and memories. But when she did speak, everyone listened. She spoke to me after I had recuperated from my journey and told me of the Sultan and all that he would require of me."

"What did he require of you? Why do the Kings, Emperors, and Sultans always want something from you?"

"An interesting question. I know you do not have Kings anymore, at least not as they were long ago. Those in power will always maintain their power by squeezing all they can from those they rule. That is their nature, Wyatt. Rulers are hardly ever gentle, noble men. They are often cruel and demanding. The thing that separates a good ruler from the bad is perception of the common man. Do you understand this? If the common man *knows* he is taken advantage of, then the ruler is a bad one. If the common man believes he is ruled by a just man, then history is kinder to him. Everything is subjective, young Wyatt. Everything is both good and bad at the same time depending on what end of the rope you find yourself on. Are you holding the noose or wearing it?"

"I guess so. I'll never have to worry about that, I think." Wyatt laughed as he scribbled a thought down in his notebook. Vasha regarded him with a queer smile.

"As you say," he offered Wyatt more wine but he shook his head. "Very well. Now, as to what was required of me. I was to teach the wives and concubines of the Sultan."

"Teach them"

"Yes. I was to teach them how to pleasure their Lord. An exciting venture to be sure." He sipped his wine with mirth in his eyes. "I spent my days relaxing by the sparkling pools, filling myself with wine and sweets. Then, as the sun rose higher in the sky, I would gather my eligible pupils and... teach."

"What made them eligible?"

"Oh, beauty, of course. They must be the most beautiful. The caregivers, these eunuchs with no sense of humor at all, picked who would be the ones I imparted my wisdom to. They had other criteria," he squinted his face as he recalled the events from the past. "Of an age, soft of speech, eagerness to please, and those with a talent for dancing or singing."

"Sounds about right."

"Yes. It was. They were eager to learn how to please their Lord Sultan. I taught them how to pleasure themselves, one another, and finally how to pleasure a man. I watched as they grew older and more confident. I watched as they moved up in the hierarchy of the Sultan's court and left our little Sparkling Oasis. Some bore the Sultan children. Others stayed with me. The new women coming in quickly took to my lessons and all was well for a long time. A very long time. I served the Sultan until he died. Then his eldest son... no wait... there was a son who died," he shrugged and took a deep drink from his cup. "Some son of the Sultan took his father's place and I continued my service. However, I was a student as well during this time."

"Oh? How so?"

"I told you of the old women who came to me, yes?" Wyatt nodded. "They taught me their form of magick. The old women taught me the symbols of protection I could paint on my body that warded evil magicks from me."

"Like the stuff you painted on Mela."

"Yes. That is precisely it. However, since I am a more complicated beast, they performed magick of a different sort in order to protect me more permanently. These scars," he leaned forward and traced the concentric circles carved into his flesh with a finger. "These the women did to me one night under the light of a blood moon. It was a night full of magick you see. Blood moons are powerful and they knew how to harness that power and transfer it to me. They chanted, called out to their Gods and ancestors as they carved my flesh using sharpened bones."

"Bones?"

"Yes. I have reason to believe the bones were from deceased relatives that they sharpened to use as tools. Most magick used for protection will require either bone or blood. Can you guess why?"

"Nope."

"Because, my simple, beautiful boy, they are the most basic tools from a time when magick was first used by humans. The crystals, the candles, the fancy spices, none of this mattered much to the Gods of old. They wanted, and still want, the blood and bones of those we hold most dear. In order to wield powerful magicks, one must be ready to use powerful tools."

"So, are you telling me that you're immune to Dark Magick now?"

Vasha sat back and studied his friend for a moment before answering. "Yes and no. Certainly, no Hag or any other creature from the darkness can catch me unawares anymore. If enough power is behind the magick, I suppose I can be over powered. However, I would be aware of it and able to defend myself. They did not cloak me as much as place a thicker shield about me. Do you understand?" Wyatt nodded. "Good. Now that you know that important piece of the story, I will tell you the price I paid for that bit of protection."

"Price?"

"Oh yes. It took many, many years for them to collect on the debt but collect they did. You see, I served for generations in this Sparkling Hall. There were Sultans who cared little for collecting concubines and therefore I sat idle for many years. Then there were those who collected women as a coin collector collects gold. It all went on for some time like this until it was time to pay my debt. As you and all those here should know, there is always a price to pay for magick. Any magick you do, be it for good or for evil, costs something.

"In my case, it cost me many years of my life. You see there was magick everywhere in those days. Old magick that called to those who craved power, money, love and revenge. I remember the day I left the Sparkling Halls, taken under the cover of darkness in wagons once again. It was a long journey. I remember most the rocky unused roads that brought us higher and higher into a mountain range."

"Where were you going?"

Vasha shrugged. "I do not remember exactly where. How could I remember such details as that? It was a deserted, barren area in a mountain. Deep caves that faced the setting sun welcomed me into their depths. There I learned of my new duties. I was no longer a member of the Sultan's household but a protector of magical secrets."

"What secrets?" Wyatt's frown deepened.

"Some books or tablets," he waved his hands in the air in frustration. "It was terribly boring work, I must admit. I was not to allow anyone into the caves until another came to relieve me of my post. If anyone came," he placed a finger on his throat and slid it across the tender flesh of his neck. "I disposed of them all."

"Wait, wait…do you remember the name of these books? Were they the Sibylline books? The ancient oracles that told the futures of kingdoms?"

"How do you know this? Who told you of these books?"

"Decker did. He told me, uh… when he told me his story about an expedition he almost went on. But everyone… everyone died."

"Oh. Well then, there you are. I killed them all most likely."

"Most likely."

"Yes. I killed many. If they were able to make their way to the mountaintop and survive the journey, they were quite robust. Nevertheless, none were or are as robust as I. It was my duty to protect the ancient scribbles of men from long ago so I did." Vasha began to laugh. "I remember once there were a few men who made the journey after a long period of not seeing another person for quite some time. The first man, I simply tossed him out of the mouth of the cave and watched him plummet to his death. All the while his little legs and arms flailed about… it was quite humorous."

"Sorry. I don't see the humor in that. At all."

"Because you are not a beast such as I, dear one. The others I killed a bit slower if that makes you feel any better."

"It doesn't"

Vasha chuckled. "Ah well. I certainly saw a humor in men working so terribly hard to climb a mountain range that would most likely kill them in order to collect ancient books that may or may not be what people say."

"What do you mean 'May or may not be what people say'?"

"What I mean, Wyatt, is that I read the dribble scratched into those tablets and papyrus. A bunch of cow manure and bloated talk of falling empires and coming storms," he took a deep drink of wine. "None of it made much sense. Oracles and fortune tellers, they are almost always frauds of some sort. I never understood the allure they held to people. However, I had a job to do and I did it."

"You just sat up in a mountain cave for... how long? Years? Decades? And killed people who came to take the books?"

"Yes. Exactly so. Until I grew bored of it all. It was dull, Wyatt," he leaned in with eyes wide. "I was utterly and completely alone. One day I awoke from my bundle of pillows and decided to leave. I packed my belongings" he gestured to the stack of boxes behind him. "Many of those here with me still. I carried everything down the mountain and left the useless books to their fates."

"Where did you go? How did you travel?"

"I quickly found a poor family willing to be my servants to see me toward my next destination. There were poor people everywhere and many were frightened just enough of me that, with the help of a little gold or silver, they were willing to conquer their fears and see to my needs. I was ready to leave that place," a sad shadow crossed his face. "I was ready to leave all I had lost behind. I wanted to disappear. I wanted to fade into an obscure part of the world and live out my days there on my own terms. Can you understand this?" Wyatt nodded.

"I decided to board a ship. I was terrified mind you but I did it anyway. I was carried to the ship in a large crate—terribly uncomfortable. There my servants left me to my own devices and I travelled for the first time on the water. Can you guess where I was bound?"

"Here? America?"

He shook his head. "No dear one. There was no America in those days. At least, not as it is colonized now. I went to a much further and much more exciting place. I left for the ancient continent of Africa."

"There seemed to be a lot of travelling in those days. You know, when we learn history, we're never told about how extensively people were able to travel."

"I suppose it has something to do with the need to create an aura of superiority for the current times." He sat back and seemed to melt into the stack of pillows behind him. "Every age of man creates a need to feel as though they've conquered the previous age. Where once there were simple stone and mud houses gave way to more comfortable wood homes with more conveniences. Where weapons were once spears and bows gave way to steel swords and shields. Now, in this current age, you are told how superior you are due to your small talking devices and electric contraptions. However, we were able to communicate and travel the world quite peacefully in those days without those contraptions. We traded with minimal conflict. We created art and music that other cultures shared amongst one another. It was simpler, yes, but it worked well."

"What makes this age any worse? What was the big shift that made things, you know, like they are now?"

"How do you see things as they are now?" Vasha's eyes narrowed and Wyatt felt the inescapable feeling he had talked himself into a corner.

"I just mean… I mean that the advances in healthcare and," his voice trailed off. "It seems like things are better really. In the long run." He fidgeted the corner of the paper.

Vasha took a long time to study his friend in the dim light of the shed. The silence created a shift in mood for both of them. He could faintly hear Wyatt breathing and outside, he could hear the birds as they carried on with their songs.

"This age is a dangerous one. More dangerous than any other age that has come and gone. Man, you infernal, beautiful creatures, have evolved into everything your ancestors fought against. Greed is your god. Total destruction of peoples and the Earth is acceptable. All honor, all hope has faded to the shadows. Your technology has warped the hearts and minds of humans. You are more machine than the original creations of long ago. Machines have no heart, Wyatt. Machines are cold and methodical, as are humans now. Truth be told, with very few exceptions, I am anxious to see how humans end up causing their own annihilation."

"You want us all to die?"

"I want the Earth to survive. In order for that to happen, humankind must fall from the precarious pedestal you have placed yourselves on. Those that are able to adapt will survive. That is what I've learned over my long life."

"That we're going to self-destruct?"

"Yes. I am anxious for that to happen. It will bring an end to the suffering of many and the rejuvenation of the Earth and the creatures that deserve to continue on it."

"Meaning we don't deserve to survive." It wasn't a question. It was probable humanity would self-destruct.

"Deserve. An interesting choice of words, my friend. If we all got what we deserved, I wonder how happy anyone would truly be. What does Mankind deserve for poisoning the oceans? What do they deserve for creating weapons that kill cities in painful and horrific ways? What do they deserve for hording water and food from those that need it most? For enslaving their brothers and sisters? I could go on but I think you understand my meaning." Vasha shifted forward and stared intently at his friend. "I do not hate your brethren. I have long loved them, as I do you. However, there comes a time where one must admit the faults in those that we love. In this case, it has been allowed to go on too long. It is time for Mankind to be reminded of their fallibility. They must remember who and what they really are in order to survive. It is not the machines that your age covets so dearly but the reason for loving them that should go on. It brings you closer together you say, yes. That is true. The idea behind it all is correct. The method is cold and unhuman. Instead of creating ways to eliminate the suffering for people of the world, this technology could be used to eliminate the cause of it. But that is the paradox of your time, isn't it? The cause of the suffering is the god of greed your kind now worships. Until that god is dead, your people will continue to suffer in unimaginable ways. This is by far the cruelest time in which I have ever lived."

A long moment passed before Wyatt cleared his throat and spoke, "It's also a great time to live, Vasha," he said softly. "People are freer than they have ever been. Love, acceptance, kindness, bravery, all of that still exists. It really does. So many of us want all the good things for our people. It's the ones in charge that don't seem too keen on the idea of keeping everyone healthy and happy."

"It isn't their job to do that, Wyatt," Vasha said in almost a whisper. "It is the people's job to care for themselves and to want to care for one another. That is what has been lost—your ability to survive on your own without a massive system in place telling you what to do at every moment of every day."

"I think we could. We haven't lost the ability to do that. We just haven't had to. But we could do it." Wyatt sounded young and naive. He had more faith in people than most other humans. He had faith because he truly believed that people were innately good and decent.

"I suppose we will have to agree to disagree on this point, dear one." Vasha said with a small smile. "But let us move on, shall we?" They both nodded. "Good. Now, where was I? Oh yes, on my way to Africa." This subject seemed to inject life back into him once more that he sat forward again with a light in his eyes. "I hate travelling by ocean. Truly detest the feeling of the ship listing here and there," he moved his hand up and down in the motion of the sea. "It's agonizingly dull business. I won't bore you with those details. Suffice it to say, I arrived in my cargo ship green with seasick and anxious to rid myself of the smelly inhabitants of that crew.

"Before long, I was carted from the docks and set down in the dead of night onto a wagon that took me out of the port town-"

"What town was it? Do you remember?"

"No. It was," he looked to be searching his mind for the answer. "It was Eastern Africa. I do not remember which city. Many of the cities that existed then no longer do. Or have not in so many centuries that they are like new again. Besides," he waved his hand. "I did not stay in the city but I was carted off into the wild. That is where I spent many years with the Swahili people. A lovely culture. Do you know of it?" Wyatt nodded. "Lovely. I'm happy to hear they were able to survive to the point of remembrance. I lived alongside them for a very long time."

"Did you have many friends there?"

Vasha shook his head. "No. I chose to stay clear of the entanglements of friendships and the like. I was tired of watching those I loved die. I was tired of being used. I simply wanted to exist."

"That doesn't sound like you at all."

The bark of laughter that escaped Vasha filled the room and made Wyatt jump. "No. It wasn't like me at all. In fact," his smile widened. "I was delighted to find they were no more afraid of me than I was of them. Many did not care to know me but the leaders of tribes and medicine men came to me and we taught one another much. In payment for my knowledge, they would bring me gems and gold. Africa was ripe with such things then. I built up quite the collection in those days. Would you like to see?"

Before Wyatt could answer, he had already begun rummaging around in the many chests, placing larger things wrapped in cloths to the side, all the while humming a strange tune to himself. After a few minutes of opening and closing wooden chests that creaked and groaned with the shifting of weight mixed with Vasha's deep voice humming his song, a pile of wrapped blobs sat in a circular pattern on the floor. Vasha, content with finding the treasures he meant to show off, set about to unwrapping them.

Wyatt gasped as Vasha unrolled emeralds as large as his fist from scratchy looking cloth. Ivory elephant tusks gilded with gold and carved with scenes of ancient men came next and it was all Wyatt could do not to grab them and run his hands over the delicate carvings. A string of pink pearls captivated his attention next. They looked too large to be real but he knew they were. Back then, there were no fake pearls, only the real thing. Each pearl was close to the size of a golf ball and made a deep clunking sounds when Vasha placed them on the floor in front of Wyatt.

"Many of the gold bracelets I wear today are from that time. See," he held two arms out in front of Wyatt's face and jingled them about making a merry sound.

"Nice. Is that a real emerald?" He couldn't take his eyes off of the green rock laying between them.

"Indeed, it is. It is heavy, here feel it." Vasha swiftly moved his jingling bracelets from the air and picked up the softball sized emerald with the other two hands. Wyatt opened his hands and felt the weight of the green gem in his hands. It was raw and such a deep green it was almost black in the center. It absorbed the dim light in the shed creating a dark rainbow in the stone's depths.

"It's beautiful." He ran his hands over the smooth parts and then over the rougher edges. I didn't think I've ever seen a real emerald before. Much less one this big."

"You admire things that are large, do you?" Vasha purred to him. Wyatt answered with a snort and placed the emerald back on the floor between them.

"What are going to do with all of this?" he gestured to the seemingly never-ending stack of chests and boxes. Vasha turned and regarded his treasure trove of goods and sighed.

"I do not know. I truly do not know." He sounded wistful and distant. His smile was faint but peaceful when he turned his attention back to Wyatt. "I do not know what I can do with all of this," he waved a hand behind him. "I believe, as I said before, that one day I could show them to the world. I would very much like everyone to see what the true history of man looks like. It was beautiful. Everywhere I went was beautiful and filled with the marvelous beings. Many were kind to me with no real reason to be. I loved so many in different ways. My things help me to remember them."

"You're hard to forget, Vasha."

"Indeed, I am." He said with a wink.

"How long were you in Africa? Any specific stories from that time that stand out to you?"

Vasha shrugged. "I have no idea really how long I was there. The world turned and times changed while I stayed in a place that was my own. I lived in a cave that was once quite important. Something about one of their Goddesses giving birth to time inside of it," he flipped his long black hair over his shoulders. "But the Swahili had many Gods, you know. In fact, I learned of a new Deity all the time. Different tribes came and went to trade with the people in my area and they brought their Gods too. Africa is a magical place. They were in touch with nature and with their gods. I enjoyed my time there very much but because I was not of that land, the chosen Deities did not speak to me."

"Did the Deities speak to them?"

"Oh yes, all of the time. The spiritual leaders within the Swahili people had strong magick and often conversed with their gods but I was never permitted to take part in that. They came to me for spells and talismans they made from my hair. It was a quiet time for me, to be honest."

"Does quiet mean you were bored?"

"Yes." They laughed. "Yes, I was incredibly bored. I kept thinking something would happen at any moment. But nothing ever did. The most interesting thing for that time came toward the end of my stay in their land."

"What? What happened?"

"Well, dear one, your ancestors came and placed men and women in bondage." He lifted his eyes to Wyatt's with raised eyebrows. "That was a dark time. At first, they were only rumors, you see. Many did not believe it was happening. We were far from where the first invaders came so the stories that made their way to us were dated and filled with impossible details. White demons that flew across the sea to steal away families seemed absurd and caused many to think their distant brethren had lost their minds. However, over the course of time, the same stories found their way to us over and over again. They were being taken away across the sea, never to be heard from again."

"God, I'd forgotten." Wyatt whispered.

"Not something the people of Africa will forget any time soon. Where I was, the people were trading with Arabs and Chinese people. So, it was only later, after the Arab slavers came and corrupted the people I had come to know, that I felt it was time to leave. You see, the Swahili people were pure and natural people. Greed was a foreign concept to many of them. Those were peaceful years for me and I was sad to see them go. I much preferred them in their natural state than that of the post trade influence. The men and women wore colored robes that often times left the women's breasts bare. I did appreciate that very much. But along came more modern clothing, or so I was told. I saw less and less of those medicine men and conduits to the old Gods. The ways of the Arabs and their new God had come with them. The movement of the monotheists had begun and monsters like me were from the old ways and better off forgotten. While I hid and enjoyed peaceful decades in the jungles, the world changed without me realizing it.

"I left my jungle home with my goods and a few servants to assist me. I wanted to catch a ship back to my homeland, back to where it all started. You see," he reclined further back and stared at the blank ceiling. "I got it in my head that perhaps I would see my brothers again after these many years if I could only go back to where we started."

"You went looking for them?"

A few silent moments went by before he answered. Perhaps he was trying to remember or perhaps he was trying to find the right words. "I made my way east first but quickly turned back. The East was ripe with slavers and my servants refused to subject themselves to that. I did not blame them a bit, after all, I knew myself how horrendous bondage can be. We went in circles really. Port after port and village after village. The people were bleeding from their land like blood from many wounds. I had nowhere to go. No real way to leave because my servants could not and would not board a ship for fear of the chains that inevitably waited for them.

"I awoke one night deserted. They had left me to, I assume, return home to where they felt safe. I was once again on my own, in a strange land."

"What did you do?"

Vasha rolled onto his side and gave Wyatt one of his most winning smiles. "That is the start of another tale, dear one. If you would forgive me, I would very much like to rest and then partake in food with my brothers. Do you mind terribly coming back tomorrow?"

Wyatt began gathering his things and smiled. "Of course not. Sure thing. I'll be back after Annabelle gets out of school.

"Lovely. Until tomorrow." He waved a hand at Wyatt as the handsome young man left the shed, closing the door with a smile. As he lay back against the pillows, he regarded the dank, brown ceiling above him. Should he tell this part of the story? Should he open that door at all? He could simply gloss over the next part, Wyatt would never know. It would be safer if he did not speak of it. But would that be lying to a man whom he respected and who cared for him? Would it be damaging to tell or not to tell it all?

Without further thought, he pulled his massive form to his feet and exited the shed. Outside the sun was setting and the night animals were starting their search for food and mates. How alike they really were. Sustenance and fucking were the basis of all things both great and small. Vasha learned to discern the natural from the unnatural world based on those simple truths alone.

"Brother," Theo's soft voice floated toward him from the shadow of a tree. Vasha looked up and saw his brother perched as if a giant, black bird on the branch of a tree. "You were long with Wyatt. Did you finish your story?"

Vasha shook his head. "No. Alas there is more to tell only…" he let his voce trail off into the night.

"Only, you do not want to tell all of your truths, is that it?"

Vasha nodded. "Yes. That is it. I am worried it will be too much truth."

"What does too much truth mean?"

"It means, dear brother, sometimes too much truth can be a bad thing. Sometimes, leaving parts of a story out is the only real way to protect them."

"Protect them or you?" Theo's yellow eyes glowed from the shadows of the tree. Vasha cocked his head to the side and pursed his lips.

"As you say, brother. As you say."

Chapter Four

"What you need all that for?" Decker called out to Vasha from behind. In his arms, he carried a handful of large candles, fresh herbs from the garden, and salt.

"Never you mind. I have business to attend to this evening."

"Setting off to summon some spirit looks to me. Ain't we got enough of all that already?"

"I am not summoning anything you idiot. These are herbs for protections and you would know this if you bothered to educated you—"

Decker waved his hands frantically in front of his face warding off his brother's scolding. "I don't much care. Was only fooling around. Why you got t'be so touchy for?" Decker scowled and stalked off back toward the house where Mela sat with Layla.

Wyatt would be arriving within the hour and Vasha wanted to take precautions before he arrived.

***

"**H**ello!" Wyatt called out as he approached the shed. Vasha stepped from behind the building giving the man a start. Holding his hand against his chest, he started to laugh. "You scared the ever lovin' Jesus out of me."

"I certainly hope not." He leaned forward and took Wyatt's face in his hands. "No, looks like there is life in you yet." He took Wyatt's hand and led him to the door of the shed. "Tonight's voyage through time will go a bit different tonight." Wyatt's eyebrows raised a fraction but he said nothing. "We will be discussing something I wish to stay between just the two of us for the time being. And it will also require a bit of…" he searched for the right word that wouldn't scare him off but still convey the point he needed to make.

"Well this sounds exciting."

"It may well be. But I need you to take this next part very seriously." He stopped and placed a hand on either of the man's shoulders. "You must do as I say, listen and write but then never read what you've written aloud. Can you do that for me?" Wyatt didn't say anything but nodded after a brief moment. "Good. Now, follow me in and take your seat. I shall follow you in when I am done."

"Done with what?"

"Closing a protection circle about the shed. It will only take a moment." He pushed Wyatt to the doors and walked around the building once more. He heard the wooden doors creak open then close with a soft thud. Good. At least he listens.

Vasha opened a velvet pouch and dipped one of his blue hands into the bag producing a finely ground mixture of red bricks, eggshells, and salt. The herbs would be added next after he had spread them around the shed. He hoped this would be enough.

After being sure he had covered a complete circle around the shed twice, Vasha entered and closed the door behind him.

"Want to tell me what that's all about?"

"You will understand shortly. Get out your paper and writing tools if you would please," he gestured to Wyatt's bag, made himself comfortable across from the man, and waited.

"Ready when you are."

"Excellent. When we left off yesterday, I almost did not speak of this part. It is painful, yes, but more than that. It is dangerous for me to recall this part of the tale out loud."

"Hence the magicks outside?"

"Yes. I will not answer any questions about this. I want you to record only what I tell you and then we can move on and, hopefully, never speak of this again. Is that clear?" Wyatt nodded slightly with a frown creasing the space between his eyes. "I did board a ship from western Africa and journeyed to a new place. I could not go home, you see, until I acquired new servants willing to travel with me. I needed constant care due to the length of the trip home. By ship, I could sail to the land of the Chinese people. They were a hardworking and spectacularly well-travelled people. I was certain I could hire servants to attend my needs, willing to take me home. The trip was long. So very long. Their tongue was strange to me but I had picked up other languages before and was soon in possession of working knowledge of their tongue in order to request the few comforts I would need.

"I had in attendance a cabin boy who never really saw me. I covered my face and hands with cloth and spoke to him from behind a veil and a barely opened door. He was not permitted into my room nor was anyone else. The Chinese were not a curious people and had lovely manners so, I was left alone as requested.

"They made many stops along the way. The silk road they called it. Pfft," he made a snorting noise that brought a smile to Wyatt's face. "Gathering silk and selling silk is dreadfully boring. I prefer to wrap it about me."

"How long was it before you reached your destination? Weeks? Months?"

Vasha shrugged. "I do not really remember. I would think a matter of months. I was nearly mad by the time we docked in southern China in some city that was massive. They unloaded the goods they brought with them but I requested a night departure. I waited in my cabin, alone, ready to disembark into this unknown land. The air smelled of fish and open fires cooking food. Hundreds of voices called out and sang songs to one another. It sounded so queer to my ears. I had become quite accustomed to living in the wild in Africa and this was a bustling metropolis in comparison.

"By the time night settled over the city and little lights twinkled across the beaches, I crept from my cabin and carried my possessions on my back like a pack mule."

"Did you know where to go?"

"No. I knew to leave the inner city at once before too many eyes gazed upon me. It is inevitable, of course, to go completely unseen. Thankfully, by the time a person could focus their eyes in the dark, I was long gone. I hurried through the shadows and out of the city. It took me most of the night just to find my way out, that is how large that particular port town was. Quite a lovely place full of unique architecture. I should like to study a map of China one of these days and try to figure out where I was."

"Would you go back? I mean, if you could?"

"No, little one. I will never return to that place." He held up a hand to stay Wyatt's coming question. "I will explain. Patience." He settled back against his pillows and fingered the tassel sewn onto the corner of one of the pillows absentmindedly. "I slept in a wet field that day, hidden from view by covering myself with blankets. The next night I ventured into the more rural areas and avoided all villages and towns. Before long, a massive mountain range loomed in the distance. I set my sights on that great prize and meant to make it my home. However, the third—no—fourth night journeying in the direction, I was abruptly stopped and turned around."

"By?"

Vasha sighed heavily. "I was walking amidst a lovely wood broken by streams babbling along from the top of the mountain when he came upon me." He stopped speaking and picked up an empty wine glass. He filled it almost to the top and brought it to his blue lips then drank it all in a few quick gulps. He picked up the bottle again and refilled his cup. "My dear, sweet eldest brother, Azul." He studied the amber liquid in his glass, watching the light dance in its depths. "He came out of nowhere," his voice was almost a whisper. "I was admiring a bush with flowers on it when I heard it, the wind rustling the trees and the sound of beating wings. For a half moment, I actually thought some large bird was coming toward me. However, as it grew from behind the misty fog of the mountain, I could see him. It was his eyes that gave him away." He drank the glass in his hands and placed the cup on the floor. "He screamed at me as he raced through the sky. I had not felt fear, real fear, in a very long time.

"I remember trying to gain control of myself and stand my ground but Azul was barreling toward me with deadly intent. He meant to snatch me between his jaws. I remember that much. I knew I had to move but my back was loaded with crates and boxes. All I could do was drop to the ground and hope he missed. He almost missed. His talons tore at my flesh on an arm and part of my back. It was painful and I cried out. I cried out his name and pleaded with him to stop."

"Did he?"

"I knew he heard me. I just know he did. However, he circled around and came back to me. His back feet pinned me to the ground and he pressed his face against mine. He had grown so large. Black and massive he was. His head was as big as my entire body. Truthfully, my brother could have killed me with one bite.

"He said to me, *'Why are you here?'* and I remember all I could do was cry. I cried like the little boy I once was because I had not realized how much I had loved him until that very moment. He asked me the same question over and over again, his voice was loud and painful that close. I reached out to him, trying to touch him and feel the warmth of his skin but he snapped at my hands causing me to bring them close to my body.

"All I wanted was for him to recognize me. I thought, if only he could remember me, he would love me again and we could be together. I was so foolish." Vasha filled his glass once more and took smaller sips this time in silence.

"He didn't recognize you? You?"

"He did. He knew exactly who I was. He knew and did not care. I can feel even now how hot his skin was and how heavy his weight as he held me down. I was and am still no match for my brother. He could have killed me straight away. Right then, I believed he would. But instead he said to me," he took a rather large drink and cleared his throat. "He said, *'I do not care if you are my brother. You are nothing to me. You will leave this place now, tonight, or I will rip you to pieces and burn your carcass until your blue skin turns black.'*" All I could do was cry. I cried out his name and begged him to remember me. *'I remember you. I curse you and my memories of you and all the rest. If you ever return, I will tear you apart...'* And then he leapt into the sky and disappeared into the fog."

"So," Vasha exhaled loudly. "I left that place bloody, broken, and sad. I traveled south, then east, then west, until I was lost. I slept where I could find shelter but kept moving. I constantly felt he was watching me. Perhaps it was my imagination or perhaps he was following me, I do not know. All I know is that I had to keep moving or else I feared he would swoop down in the dead of night and devour me as he promised me he would. I decided to try to take the long way by land back to my home. It would have been a journey worth taking."

"That's a really long way to go."

"Yes," he finished the wine from his glass." I did find my way through mountain passes and into what was once a land I knew. So much had changed. The people were the same and the food was the same but the Gods changed everything. Gone were the old Gods and the new Christian and Muslim Gods were warring with one another. A bloody business that all was. I am not like Decker, I do not relish a fight if not absolutely necessary. I eluded the battles and avoided the religious zealots which brought me back to the deserts and tribal people I once knew."

"Where exactly was this?"

"Oh, by this time, perhaps somewhere near Turkey." He shrugged. "I went in search of households I once knew, or that once knew me, but many had been abandoned long ago. Only one I found remembered the tales of long ago about the blue monster that could seduce any man or woman he came across. The father of the house, the Sultan, had adopted a new religion and all harems and pleasure houses were closed for impropriety. The servants informed me in whispers that my presence would not be welcomed by the Sultan but perhaps his son would. So, I was asked to wait in an abandoned house where once a beautiful garden thrived. As I sat there amongst the spoiled greenery and stench of rotten fruit, I finally had a chance to catch my breath."

"Alone again, eh?"

"Yes, alone again. Once more without a home and rejected by those that once loved me. I waited there in that abandoned house for weeks when finally, one night, a caravan of men on horseback approached. I watched them from a hiding place behind a crumbling wall. I was dirty, you see. I was hungry and alone. I hated that feeling.

"The men climbed down from their large horses and looked around casually. I wasn't sure why they were there and did not want them to see me if they meant me harm. I was lacking another hiding place and could not disappear as easily as I once had because there seemed to be people every direction I turned. So, I hid. I watched as they walked about, seemingly there for a rest or to speak in private as the abandoned building was far from the nearest abode."

"How many were there? What happened next?"

"I don't remember how many exactly. There were, let's see," he closed his eyes and tapped his chin with a blue finger. "Seven or eight of them. Yes. Seven or eight. That is including a few servants, of course. So, not many."

Wyatt wrote as fast as he could and nodded for Vasha to continue.

"The men found places to sit and it seemed they were there to rest. I sat back and waited for them to leave. Little did I know that one of the servants was tasked with finding me. He had told his Lord, the Sultan's youngest son, that I was here and they came to find me.

"The servant came noisily through my hiding place whispering that he was there in peace and his Lord wanted a word. I waited though, I waited for the sun to fall and the men were forced to light fires in order to see. Then I crept from my hiding place and stood as tall and as imposing as I could. Even in my disheveled state, I was quite impressive." Vasha smiled and took another sip from his cup. "The men smiled at me and treated me with enough curtesy that I felt certain they had not come to try and harm me. I had had quite enough of pain, thank you very much. I wanted to return to a comfortable life in the service of a great Lord and Sultan."

"And did you? Go into his service?"

Vasha swished a mouthful of wine around in his mouth before swallowing it. "Yes. In time. The youngest brother had plans to leave his homeland for the adventures of the New World. By that time, it was vogue for the wealthy and the desperate to make their way in the land of savages and wild country. The Sultan's son had a plan to carry as much of his own riches as he could across the seas to the New World where he planned to revive the old ways and start anew. Out from under his father's religious disapproval."

"Finally! We're coming to the present time, yes?"

"Well," he tilted his elegant head back and considered. "It was well over a hundred years ago. Almost two hundred. So, we are almost to current time. Let me see, where was I?"

"You were making plans to go across the sea with the Sultan's son."

"Oh yes. Yes, that took some planning and finally I was aboard a ship bound for the New World. However, the voyage took a very long time. We made many stops along the way picking up silks, spices, treasures and all such things. But the day came when we pulled into the port of New Orleans and a whole new adventure began for me."

"I love New Orleans! Mela and I just went not too long ago."

"From what I've heard it hasn't changed much and that makes me happy. I like when things stay the same and retain their ancient wonder."

"It has some changes but they go to great lengths to keep the history alive there. It's one of the things I love the most about it."

"Indeed. Now, about my arrival into New Orleans; I was not invited to join the parade down the main streets of the city. I was loaded into a crate once more and carried along behind the Sultan's son and his entourage of servants, women, and friends. We settled into a large house downtown. It was a lively meeting place but they did not invite outsiders to join them. I was given quarters that were a bit cramped for my size but nonetheless acceptable.

"Night after night, the Sultan's sons and their entourage held parties that harkened back to the days of old. In truth, they were quite good at reviving the ancient days of pleasure houses. However, this new generation," he swatted away the memory. "They were not truly there for the pleasure. It was once that the art of pleasuring another was sacred, something to be savored and enjoyed. These men, nay, boys, were nothing of that sort. They were selfish and cruel. Often the cruelty bled into their sexual appetites and we both know I had enough of that from my past."

"I understand."

"Yes. You might," Vasha cleared his throat and readjusted his position on the floor leaning forward. "I was not exactly a prisoner there, you see, but I was beholden to them. I relied on them for food, for protection, and from discovery. The New World had no monsters such as me. Any glimpse of me in that place and I would have been hunted and disemboweled in the streets."

"You're probably right."

"I know I was. They often threatened to leave me if I did or said anything to offend the bratty Sultan sons. It was unavoidable, I suppose."

"What was?"

"Me offending them," he said with a smile. "I do not even remember how the argument began. Most likely something trivial. Nevertheless, I was threatened one too many times. I could not stay there anymore. I told them this and they laughed at me. I do not like to be laughed at." A deep frown marred his flawless blue forehead. "They threw things at me, called me names. I grew angry, of course, and it…. escalated."

"Escalated? What does that mean?"

Vasha's frown disappeared and instantly transformed into a smile. "I killed them. I killed every single one of them."

"Oh."

"I was not necessarily angry, I simply wanted to leave but I grew angry very quickly when they told me I was not permitted to leave. Ever. A large, mustached man told me that I would leave in pieces or not at all. I did not appreciate that threat very much."

"I don't blame you. But you killed them? All of them?"

"Every man, woman, and child in that home, I tore to pieces." The shed went quiet. The sounds from outside were muted through the wood walls. Somewhere, the sound of voices wafted through the air. One of them laughed. These sounds mixed with the thumping of Wyatt's heartbeat in his ears. "This shocks you? Truly? I told you, I would never allow myself to be a captive ever again. Perhaps I could have fought my way out and left some alive, yes. But that is not my way."

"Children?"

"Yes. The children were difficult to kill, I will admit. They were being used for abominable things and their lives were worth nothing living as they were. They would not be capable of caring for themselves in the new world where they did not speak the language. What I did was a mercy—for them. The others died rather horribly, I am afraid.

"The first few I simply ripped apart. Easy since they were drunk and asleep through most of it. I remember the blood. It was everywhere," he studied his hands in the dim light. "The blood covered all of my hands and arms. It painted the walls and my skin. It dripped through the doorway, that is how the locals discovered the carnage. The blood was flowing so freely it ran into the street."

"So," Wyatt cleared his throat and pretended to write something as he searched for the right words. "Do you ever feel guilty? You know, guilty for what you did?"

Vasha frowned, shrugged his muscular shoulders, and sighed. "Perhaps I should but I do not. Death for someone like me is," he moved his hands as though flicking the thought away. "Common. People die every day and the manner of their death is of little importance."

Wyatt scribbled into his notebook and stayed uncharacteristically silent.

"I can see this bothers you so I shall be brief. I left the Sultan's house but only after I buried the youngest son alive in the back yard. I packed my belongings, added a bit more to my treasures, and left before the sun came up.

"Before long, I was lost in the western wilderness of the New World. The native people were afraid of me but accorded me every hospitality along the way. I wanted the coast, you see. The wild coasts of the Western New World. There, I heard tales of trees larger than mountains and caves overlooking the ocean. That is where I finally found solitude with the smell of the sea and no humans to enslave or mistreat me."

"Until Theo found you."

"Yes, until my brother found me." He sighed. "I had many years of quiet solitude where I enjoyed the natural wonders of a green and lustrous world. Then one day, I felt a familiar presence. Theo came to tell me of his reunion with our wild brother and of a young witch whom he had come to love with all his heart."

"Our Mela."

"Yes. The lovely little witch destined to fight the evil that surrounds us. Destined to fight. Destined to die most likely."

"What?" Wyatt's voice was loud and echoed in the small space. "You think she'll die?"

Vasha sat still moving only his yellow eyes to meet Wyatt's. "It is the fate of all, dear one. Her path takes her down a dangerous road and I cannot see this story ending with her happily ever after as the stories say." He broke his gaze and looked around his home with a mild look of concern. "However, I suppose with the right help it might be possible to save some of you. But all…" he shook his head. "I hope you know that I have deep love for everyone here. Our little family has become precious to me. Nevertheless, I am a realist, Wyatt. We cannot fight this large of a battle and come away unscathed." His voice turned softer. "You understand that, Wyatt? You understand that in war people die? Make no mistake my friend, we are at war and it will get much worse before the end." Wyatt nodded but Vasha knew the truth. He did not understand. Not really. However, he would and very soon.

Epilogue

Under the light of the moon, Vasha walked with Theo on his heels. They could do this, walk in silence, and feel perfectly at ease. Words were not necessary between the two brothers. The crisp autumn breeze tickled his skin as his brother placed his furry hand in one of his.

"Oy. Wait for me you long legged gits." The sound of crunching dead leaves beneath Decker's feet broke the tranquility of their walk.

"Brother." Vasha nodded his head in his brother's direction.

Decker huffed and puffed holding his side as he approached the pair. "I've been calling for you," he took a deep breath. "Didn't you hear me?"

Vasha joined Theo in a shared smile. "Yes, but we know how much you like to scream and run so we thought we would oblige."

"Dicks." He kicked a pile of leaves and watched them flutter through the air. "What you two up to?"

"Enjoying the evening, brother." Theo purred. He held out his other hand in offering to Decker. Reluctantly, he took the hand offered matching their stride through the open field.

"What troubles you, Dektrios?" Theo's words were almost a whisper. Both brothers turned to look at him knowing he would not intentionally seek them out without a purpose.

"Mela, she's uh…"

"We are aware of her inquiries. I have warned her against it. Fear not."

"Fear not?" he snorted. "You don't know her like I do. Neither of you. She might tell you she ain't talking about him anymore but she's thinking about him. Bet your ass she is."

The brothers continued on in silence. They all knew he was right. Mela would not let the thought of Azul go, a real threat to those she loves, easily. Each one of them contemplated the situation but never let go of one another's hands.

"What will come will come." Vasha said as the shadows of the night crept from the surrounding tree line. "We cannot control it. We know this. The only thing we can do is to be here and be ready for what happens next."

"Yes," Theo said. "We cannot leave no matter what. They need our protection. They need Vasha's wisdom." He squeezed his brother's hand. "They will need your strength, Decker." He turned and smiled a toothy smile.

"We will need you as well, sweet brother. We will need you to hold us together when the fighting begins." Both Decker and Vasha stepped a little closer to their black-haired brother. In silence they walked on, knowing the war had only just begun and each one of them hoped for a miracle to save those they love.

About Mel Massey

Mel Massey lives in Washington State with her family. She is the author of the EARTH'S MAGICK series as well as SERVANT OF THE BLOOD, GETAWAY, and other short stories in the paranormal and supernatural genres. Mel is a member of the International Thriller Writer's Association. For updates on this and future works, visit her website: www.melmassey.com.

Social Media Links:

Website: www.melmassey.com

Facebook:
www.facebook.com/melmasseyauthor

Twitter:
https://twitter.com/melmmassey
@melmmassey

If you enjoyed this story, check out these other Solstice Publishing books by Mel Massey:

Earth's Magick Book One ~ Earth ~

Life in Trinity Hills, Texas goes from normal to deadly for Mela Malone. Whenever Mela falls asleep, a mysterious creature, called The Hag, tries to kill her. What begins as dabbling in protective spells from an ancient Grimoire, leads to her initiation into an ancient order of warrior witches known as the Elementai. Mela learns war is coming with The Darkness and the Hag is only one of the evil creatures in its service. As an Elementai, Mela learns it's her duty to find four part-human sisters who can help defeat the evil that threatens to return to the world. With every new discovery, Mela uncovers ancient secrets that complicate her quest further. As war approaches, everyone must make a choice - fight with the Elementai for all life on Earth, or fight for The Darkness…

https://bookgoodies.com/a/B00HQP90AS

Decker

In this first companion novel to the Earth's Magick series, Decker tells his incredible, and sometimes painful, life story. For over 2,000 years, he has fought to survive and find his place in this ever-changing world. Beginning in a remote village in ancient Saudi Arabia, he takes the reader with him to Egypt, Rome, Gaul, Ireland, Scotland, Africa, and finally to the New World. Earth's Magick readers will relive Decker's incredible adventures and his most intimate secrets.

https://bookgoodies.com/a/B00KLMEP8U

Earth's Magick Book Two ~ Water ~

Mela Malone is one of the most powerful Witches in Texas. While learning how to defeat Evil using magick, and a sword, the unexpected departure of two of her closest friends disrupts the balance of her world. Meanwhile, a new threat comes to Trinity Hills, Texas that puts even the innocent townspeople in danger. Mela must step up and defend, not only those she loves, but the entire town. Both old and new friends bring additional complications into her chaotic life...especially since one of them is a handsome Witch on a mission of his own.

https://bookgoodies.com/a/B00OPDPL3E